"I want you, Zach, ... there's no room. We can't."

"Oh, but we can," Chelsea corrected, drawing his mouth to hers.

Sensations flooded through him as her mouth moved on his, her tongue probing. Her heat, her scent, her taste, swirled in his head until he couldn't separate them. All night long, he'd watched while she danced in other men's arms. Now she was his. Slipping his fingers beneath the thin straps on her shoulders, he began to push them aside.

"No." Chelsea drew back. "You can't take off my top. I'm sewn into it. If you loosen it, the skirt won't stay up."

"Damn the skirt," Zach said. "I need to touch you. I've been waiting to touch you all day. And you dragged me into this closet...."

"To have my wicked way with you." Settling back on the shelf, Chelsea grinned seductively. Then, taking his hands, she ran them along her thighs, pushing the skirt out of the way. "Now, Zach, don't tell me you're complaining...."

Dear Reader,

What happens when a single girl navigating her way through the dating scene in a big city gets a little help from a skirt that has the power to draw men like a magnet?

That's what the heroine of *Moonstruck in Manhattan* is about to discover!

Sick of the singles scene in the Big Apple, Chelsea Brockway has sworn off dating, period! From now on, she's just going to write about it. And she sees her friend's supposed man-magnet skirt as her ticket to a lucrative contract with *Metropolitan* magazine. All she has to do is prove to Zach McDaniels, the sexy new editor-in-chief, that the skirt works. And it does, all too well....

If you enjoyed *Moonstruck in Manhattan,* don't miss the rest of the SINGLE IN THE CITY miniseries: *Tempted in Texas* by Heather MacAllister in January 2002, and *Seduced in Seattle* by Kristin Gabriel in February 2002. In the meantime, I hope Zach and Chelsea's romantic adventures will brighten your holiday season.

Happy Holidays!

Cara Summers

P.S. I love to hear from readers. Write to me at P.O. Box 718, Fayetteville, NY, 13066. And check out our Web site at www.singleinthecity.org!

Books by Cara Summers

HARLEQUIN TEMPTATION	HARLEQUIN DUETS
813—OTHERWISE ENGAGED	40—MISTLETOE & MAYHEM
	56—THE LIFE OF RILEY

MOONSTRUCK IN MANHATTAN
Cara Summers

ISBN 0-373-25960-8

MOONSTRUCK IN MANHATTAN

Copyright © 2001 by Carolyn Hanlon.

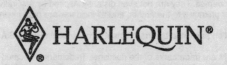

TORONTO • NEW YORK • LONDON
AMSTERDAM • PARIS • SYDNEY • HAMBURG
STOCKHOLM • ATHENS • TOKYO • MILAN • MADRID
PRAGUE • WARSAW • BUDAPEST • AUCKLAND

To my Aunt Kathleen—for introducing me
to Nancy Drew and the Bobbsey Twins when I was
seven. And for always being there for me—
in the best of times and in the worst of times.

To my Uncle Jimmy, too—and to the romance
that you and Aunt Kathleen have lived together.

I love you both.

ISBN 0-373-25960-3

MOONSTRUCK IN MANHATTAN

Copyright © 2001 by Carolyn Hanlon.

_____Prologue_____

"THE BRIDE is _not_ going to throw her bouquet." Chelsea made a wide sweep with her foot under the table and located the sandals she'd kicked off earlier. Her feet were killing her. Getting married on a California beach at sunrise sounded romantic. But it wasn't so much fun when the bridesmaids had to walk around the rest of the day with sand in their shoes.

"What are you talking about? She _has_ to throw her bouquet!" Gwen said. "Torrie is the most conventional person I know."

"I might even get up the energy to make a try for it. That is if I could believe catching a bunch of posies would get me a decent date," Kate said.

"A date? What's that?" Gwen asked.

"It's been that long, huh?" Chelsea asked and then joined in the laughter. After rooming together during their senior year in college, she and Kate and Gwen had each gone on to pursue career goals in separate cities. But they'd managed to keep in touch by phone. Chelsea couldn't help recalling how often they'd had similar conversations over the years, discussing the dating wasteland they'd encountered in the big city.

And the dangers, she thought as a little band of pain tightened around her heart.

Loud cheers and whistles drew their attention to a raised platform at the far end of the dance floor where the groom was removing the garter from the bride's leg.

"You've got to be wrong, Chels," Kate said starting to rise from the table. "The bouquet comes right after the garter."

Chelsea grabbed her arm. "But it's not the bouquet she's going to toss. It's the *skirt*."

Her two friends stared at her, comprehension, surprise and finally amusement flickering across their faces.

"Not the man-magnet skirt?" Gwen asked.

"The one she picked up on that island during her cruise?"

"You got it," Chelsea said. They'd all listened countless times to the story of how Torrie's cruise ship, blown off course by a storm, had dropped anchor at a small out-of-the-way island, and how she'd found this little shop where an elderly seamstress had sold her a special skirt. According to the woman, each spring, the old ladies of the island gathered on a moonlit beach to spin the fibers of the *lunua* plant into thread. Any woman who wore a garment woven out of this thread that had been supposedly "kissed by moonlight" would draw men like a magnet. And one of those men would be her soul mate.

Privately, Chelsea had always wondered if those island women had been sitting on that beach smoking the fibers and spinning stories instead of thread. While the skirt was a great basic black that fit Torrie perfectly, none of them had ever been able to see anything special about the "fibers" or the "thread." Still, Torrie swore by it, crediting the skirt with attracting men every time she put it on. And now she claimed it had brought her new husband to her.

"You're putting us on," Gwen said, glancing at the bride and groom. "She's not going to toss the skirt. She doesn't even have it up there with her."

"She's wearing it," Chelsea said. As if on cue, Torrie began to hike up the yards of satin cascading from her waist. "She told me she wasn't going to take it off until he said, 'I do.'"

When the three of them pushed back their chairs and rose as one, Kate said, "This is not a very good testimonial to being single in the city. We've all got to be desperate to believe in a moon-kissed skirt!"

"I want to catch it," Chelsea said.

Gwen and Kate turned to stare at her.

"You? We thought you'd sworn off men after Boyd the bum."

Kate's elbow cut Gwen short. "We're not going to mention his name ever again. Remember? A low-life cad like that does not deserve one more minute of our time. And I think it's great that you're going to throw yourself back into the dating jungle, Chels. At least one of us should be out there."

"Oh, but I'm not... I mean...," Chelsea paused, touched by the concern she saw in her friends' eyes. Truthfully, she didn't want the skirt to attract men. She had entirely different plans for Torrie's man-magnet skirt. But Kate and Gwen looked so happy for her...

"You go, girl." Gwen said. "If she tosses it our way, we'll swat it to you."

"Love you," Chelsea said, throwing her arms around them for a quick, three-way hug.

By the time they'd elbowed their way in front of the other single women who'd crowded onto the dance floor, Torrie's wedding dress was back in place and she'd begun to swing the skirt over her head like a lasso.

As Chelsea watched it move in a circle, she thought she saw a silvery flash of light like the glitter of the moon on the rippling surface of the sea. Then suddenly, the skirt was sailing through the air. Leaping high, she snagged just the edge of the fabric between her fingers.

A cheer went up around her and a funny little tingle shot through her as she clutched the skirt close to her chest.

A special plant and the kiss of moonlight? Ridiculous. However, a skirt that supposedly acted like a magnet on men was just the kind of gimmick she needed to sell her next article to *Metropolitan* magazine.

Glancing down at it, she thought she caught just a glint of silver again, and an image filled her mind—she was sitting behind an editor's desk at *Metropolitan*, pen in hand, writing a regular column.

That was her dream.

It was just her imagination that for a split second she'd seen a man in that chair with her.

1

"TAKE IT OFF. Take it all off!" Leaning over the top of the bar, Daryl shot Chelsea one of his five hundred-megawatt smiles.

She stared at her roommate as she pulled her coat more tightly around her. "Right here? In the middle of the restaurant?" She waved a hand toward the wall of windows separating them from a steady stream of pedestrian traffic. "With half of Manhattan looking on?"

"Sweetie, you said it couldn't wait until I got off work."

"It can't," Chelsea said. "I wouldn't have bothered you here if it wasn't an emergency. Couldn't you take a break and we could go into one of the private dining rooms?"

Daryl rolled his eyes as he swiped a cloth over the top of the gleaming bar. His long dark hair was pulled back and fastened at the nape of his neck and small gold hoops hung from his ears. "Christmas is exactly a week away. And while I know that it's not your favorite holiday, the rest of the world goes all out for it. The private dining rooms are booked solid. If you want my help with that skirt, you're going to have to unveil it right here, right now, before the place gets really busy."

Tearing her gaze away from Daryl, Chelsea glanced quickly around the trendy eating spot. At eleven-forty-five in the morning, the bar was still empty. In the main dining room, a few of the tables were already filled, and the maître d' was seating a couple at a nearby table.

"Chels," Daryl prompted. "It's not like I'm asking you to strip. Just take off your coat. Isn't it time that you gave that man-magnet skirt a little test drive?"

Still, Chelsea didn't remove her coat. As ridiculous as it might be, the whole idea of wearing the skirt in public made her a little nervous. It had hung in her closet for three weeks, ever since she'd gotten home from the wedding. She hadn't even tried it on until this morning when she'd gotten the phone call from *Metropolitan* magazine. The editor had asked her to wear the skirt when she came in to sign the contract.

Could a "lucky" skirt help a single girl attract men in Manhattan?

That was the question that had sold not one, but three articles. Now it had a bubble of panic growing in her stomach. She wasn't quite sure what bothered her most—the slim possibility that the skirt might actually work or the more certain probability that it wouldn't.

"What's up, Chels?" Ramón asked, wiping his hands meticulously on a towel as he hurried toward them. "I'm in the middle of creating a soufflé, but I got the message that there's some kind of emergency."

"Chelsea has a skirt problem," Daryl explained.

"A skirt problem!" Ramón—her cousin who had sworn her to secrecy about the fact that he had been born Raymond—narrowed his eyes and glared at her. Standing at six feet three inches and weighing in at over two hundred pounds, he looked as though he'd be more comfortable wearing shoulder pads and a football jersey. But Ramón was perfectly at home in a chef's hat and apron. His four years in the marines allowed him to run his kitchen like a well-oiled military machine. "You dragged me away from my soufflé to solve a skirt problem?"

"Calm down. I need you to take my place behind the bar so that I can work a little fashion magic," Daryl explained. "You know what a fanatic our friend Pierre is."

Ramón glanced at his watch. "I can give you sixty seconds. No more."

Winking at Chelsea, Daryl exchanged places with Ramón. "You may be able to run your kitchen like a boot camp, but we artists can't be rushed."

Chelsea bit down on the inside of her cheek to prevent a grin. In spite of the fact that they were total opposites and reminded her of Neil Simon's odd couple, Daryl and Ramón were the best of friends. She'd met Daryl while waitressing at a tiny Italian restaurant in the village. Ramón had fixed her up with the job when she'd first arrived in Manhattan.

Ramón had been a line cook and Daryl had been bartending part-time while taking classes at the fashion institute. Soon, the three of them had begun spending most of their free time together, talking about their dreams of making it big in New York. Six months ago, each bearing scars from their battles in the Manhattan dating scene, they'd moved into an apartment together and formed a "singles club." For the length of time that it took them to establish themselves in their chosen careers, they'd each sworn to steer clear of any serious relationships. If they even went out on a date, they had to pay a twenty-dollar fine.

"Okay. Off with the coat!" Daryl said, snapping his fingers. "And stand over there by the windows so that I can get the full effect."

Chelsea shot one more glance around the dining room. Besides the man and woman seated a short distance from the entrance to the bar, there was a group of four women just arriving at the maître d's desk. It wouldn't be long before the restaurant was filled, so it was now or never.

If only she didn't feel so torn about the skirt. In spite of what she'd let Gwen and Kate believe, the last thing she wanted in her life right now was a man. She hadn't been able to forget that strange feeling that had run through her when she'd caught the skirt—nor the image of that man sitting in the chair with her.

"Fifty seconds and counting," Ramón said.

Drawing in a deep breath, Chelsea pulled off her coat and tossed it on a bar stool. When she glanced down at the skirt, her stomach plummeted. It looked just as bad as it had in the mirror that morning, sagging at her waist and falling well below her knees. A man magnet, it wasn't! Men were much more likely to take one look and run in the opposite direction. That was not going to give her the three articles she'd promised to deliver to *Metropolitan*.

"It's too big," Ramón announced. "And you now have forty seconds."

"Stop making me feel like I'm on Cape Canaveral," Daryl said as he circled Chelsea. "I think if I just nip it in at the waist and shorten it about six inches..."

"No, you can't make any permanent alterations. The island woman who sold it to Torrie said that might interfere with the skirt's power."

Daryl's brows shot up. "I thought you didn't believe in all that moonlight and magic mumbo jumbo?"

"I don't. I mean, I don't really believe it, but I've just been offered a three article contract with *Metropolitan* magazine, and it would be nice if *something* happened when I wear this skirt."

"You sold your idea!" Daryl gave her a quick, hard hug. "Hooray for you!"

Keeping one eye on his watch, Ramón gave her a thumbs-up salute. "Way to go, Chels! Thirty seconds."

"Lighten up, Ramón. We should be opening a bottle of champagne."

"No, he's right, Daryl. You both have to get back to work, and I'm on my way over to *Metropolitan* to sign the contract right now. I just thought before I did, I should try the skirt on—" Pausing, she glanced around the restaurant again. The couple the maître d' had seated were totally engrossed in their conversation, and the only people even looking at the skirt were her two roommates. She breathed a small sigh of relief. "What do you think?"

"I think it's a bust," Ramón said. "If that skirt has any special power, wouldn't Daryl and I be affected by it?"

"Heavens no," Daryl said with a dismissive wave of his hand. "I'm not attracted to women and you're her cousin, Ramón. I'm sure that makes a difference."

"The secret to any successful endeavor is planning. Perhaps you should have tried the skirt out before you sold the idea, Chels."

The sympathetic look that Daryl shot her nearly made her smile. Ramón's little planning lecture was one they'd both heard before. Frequently. And it certainly had merit. If she ever found the time to follow Ramón's advice, she wouldn't have to go through life improvising her way out of scrapes. Like the one she was almost in right now.

"Torrie said it didn't have the same effect on all men." She glanced down at the skirt again. "Right now, I'd be happy if it could elicit something other than raucous laughter. I look pathetic in this."

"Not to worry," Daryl said as he slipped his hands beneath her sweater. "We'll just use a runway model trick. Hand me the stapler, Ramón."

Ramón grabbed the stapler from its position near the computer and slapped it into Daryl's hand. "Twenty seconds."

"A little tuck here...now one on this side...and one in the back. The trick is to make sure the tucks are small so they're not so noticeable. There." Daryl passed the stapler back to Ramón. "Now the tape."

Ramón slapped the tape dispenser into Daryl's hand. "Ten seconds."

"This part would be easier if you could slip the skirt off," Daryl said to Chelsea.

"You've got to be kidding."

With a shrug, Daryl dropped to his knees and reached up under her skirt.

"Enemy approaching at three o'clock," Ramón said in a stage whisper.

Chelsea and Daryl turned in unison to see the maître d' bearing down on them. He was a short man with a receding hairline and a mustache that curled up at the ends even when he was frowning. He reminded Chelsea of Hercule Poirot.

"What is going on here?" he asked in an accent that Chelsea pegged as wannabe French.

"Just a little fashion emergency, Pete," Daryl said.

"The name is Pierre. How many times do I have to tell you that?"

"We'll be done in a sec." Ripping off a piece of tape, Daryl folded up a section of Chelsea's skirt and secured it.

"Stop that right now. First you're fondling her under her sweater, and now you have your hand up her skirt! What will the customers think?" Pierre asked, then raised his eyes to pin Chelsea with a glare. "Miss, I'll have to ask you to..."

Even as his sentence trailed off, Chelsea glanced past him to the couple seated just beyond the entrance to the bar. The woman wasn't staring at her. But the man was. On second thought, he was scowling. She felt Daryl's hands reach under her skirt again.

"Daryl, I think you'd better—"

"Miss," Pierre paused to clear his throat. "I'd like to apologize for the behavior of our bartender. If you would allow me the pleasure of seating you at one of our best tables, I can offer you a complimentary lunch."

Chelsea stared at the maître d'. A moment ago, he'd been frowning. Now he was beaming a smile at her and offering her a free lunch.

"Turn," Daryl said as he ripped off another strip of tape.

"Customers are looking at us. I don't want you to get fired," Chelsea said in a low tone. She didn't want him to get hurt either. The scowling man was beginning to look dangerous.

"I just have one more section to fix. Turn."

Even after she did as she was told, Chelsea felt the scowling man's eyes boring into the back of her neck. Her skin had started to prickle. She could have sworn she felt that gaze move right down her body to where Daryl was fastening the last bit of tape to her hem.

"YOU HAVEN'T HEARD a word I've said."

Zach tore his gaze from the woman at the bar and

fastened it on his favorite aunt. He was sure that Miranda McDaniels would have been his favorite hands down, even if she hadn't been his only aunt. From the time he was a child, she had personified the word flamboyant to him. She was also one of the kindest and most generous people he knew. "Yes, I have. You're trying to convince me that—"

The rest of his reply was cut off by the arrival of a waiter to take their drink orders. Zach managed to suppress a smile when his aunt ordered a martini straight up with a cherry. The waiter never missed a beat as he scribbled it on his pad.

"And you, sir?"

"I'll have bottled water."

As soon as the waiter had moved away, Zach grinned at Miranda. "Let me guess. The cherry will go with your outfit."

"Exactly," Miranda said. "Not to mention my nails."

Not many women could carry off the bright red wool suit and the wide-brimmed hat, but his aunt could. On impulse, he took her hand and raised it to his lips.

"You're trying to distract me."

"Am I succeeding?"

Miranda sighed. "Have you heard anything I've said?"

"You're trying to make me believe that my father really intended for me to run *Metropolitan* magazine. But it's not going to work. The bottom line is that he left it to you in his will because he was sure that I couldn't be trusted with it."

Miranda McDaniels sighed and shook her head. "You're a lot like him, you know. Stubborn, opinionated—" She broke off her sentence to follow the direction of her nephew's gaze. "Well, well. No wonder you aren't paying two cents worth of attention to anything I've said. She's very pretty."

"The bartender would agree with you," Zach said. "He hasn't been able to keep his hands off her since she took her coat off. Of course, that skirt hides nothing. She might as well be naked."

Miranda's eyes narrowed. "What are you talking about? She's fully clothed. In fact, that skirt is too long."

"Can't you see her legs?" Zach asked. They were much longer than he'd imagined and he'd been thinking about them quite a bit since she'd taken off her coat and stepped toward the window. With the light behind it, he could see right through the thin material of the skirt. She wasn't very tall, but below her waist she was all legs. A little fantasy of just how those legs might feel wrapped around him had begun to play and replay itself in his mind. He couldn't seem to shake it loose. He felt exactly the way he had several times as a teen, totally paralyzed by a hormone surge.

"I've heard of men undressing women with their eyes, but this is the first time I've actually witnessed it taking place," Miranda said.

Zach tore his gaze away from the woman at the bar

to find his aunt laughing at him. He felt the heat rise in his cheeks. That hadn't happened since he was a teenager, either.

She leaned closer to him. "If you'd like I could make a quiet exit stage left and you could go introduce yourself to that young lady."

Zach frowned but he couldn't prevent his eyes from returning to the woman in the bar. "A lady would hardly be wearing a skirt like that. Nor would she allow a man to fondle her in a public place."

Miranda's eyes widened. "I don't think I've ever heard you speak about a woman in quite that judgmental way before. You sound like your brother."

"Ouch!" The corners of his mouth curved as he pantomimed pulling an arrow out of his heart. "Way to hurt a guy."

"Drastic measures were called for. One stuffy prude for a nephew is all I can handle."

"Speaking of Jerry, how does our esteemed congressman feel about your decision to put me in charge at *Metropolitan* magazine?" Zach was sure it must have come as an unpleasant shock to his older brother that Miranda was going to do what his father had failed to do—hand the publishing part of his empire over to the black sheep of the family. "He must have given you a hard time at the board meeting."

"On the contrary. He had no choice but to support my recommendation. If he'd made any strenuous objection, it might have looked as if he was stabbing his brother in the back." Miranda's lips curved. "You have to be very careful not to do that when your campaign for public office is based on restoring family values."

"And they all agreed to let me break the news to the editorial staff?"

"Absolutely. It's your magazine now. You call the shots."

My magazine. He played the phrase over in his mind, liking the sound of it. Running *Metropolitan* had been a dream of his since he'd been a child. Unfortunately, it had not been part of his father's dream for him. Jeremiah McDaniels, Sr. had wanted his sons to run for public office. He could train people to run his businesses, he said. He wanted his sons in positions of power. Zach's brother had gone along with the plan. He hadn't. "Jerry can't be happy."

Miranda shrugged and smiled. "He didn't like it much when you made Harvard Law Review either. That was one distinction that eluded him. Your father was proud of you that day."

"One day in thirty years." Zach shook his head. "But he wasn't proud enough of me to give me a job at *Metropolitan* after I graduated. And he definitely wasn't proud of me when I turned down the position he'd lined up for me at that prestigious law firm." He could still recall his father's exact words, ones that he'd heard over and over as he'd been growing up. *Can't you do anything right?* "Let's face it, Aunt Miranda, there just isn't enough evidence for you to win your case here. My father did not want me at *Metropolitan*."

"All right." She threw up her hands in surrender. "I give up. Serves me right for trying to argue with a Harvard law man. From now on, I'm just going to enjoy having lunch with my favorite nephew."

Zach reached for her hands. "I don't want you to think I'm not grateful, Aunt Miranda. I know that you really had to go to bat for me with the board. They can't have liked all the job-hopping I've done since law school."

"You don't need to thank me. What might look like job-hopping to some looks entirely different to me. I'm sure that while you were consulting for those newspapers in San Francisco, Chicago and Atlanta, you were gaining experience and making contacts that will prove very valuable to *Metropolitan*."

Zach's eyes narrowed as he studied her. "What makes you think that?"

Miranda squeezed his fingers before releasing them. "I've known you since you were a little boy. Even then you were a planner—never making a move until you weighed all the options. I can't wait to hear what you've planned for the magazine. It's been going downhill since your father became ill, I'm afraid."

"I'm going to make changes—in the focus, even in the intended audience."

Miranda threw back her head and laughed. "Why am I not surprised?"

Zach leaned toward her. "It's what I've always wanted to do, but Dad would never have allowed it. He always thought power lay in the hands of the government. But the real power is in ideas. I want *Metro-politan* to become a forum where the respected writers and thinkers of our time can discuss ideas."

Miranda lifted her water glass in a toast. "Then go to it. And see if you can catch the eye of our waiter. We should be toasting this with the drinks we ordered."

Zach shifted his gaze to the bar and stared. The bartender had his hand up the woman's skirt again. "Look at that. Someone should put a stop to it."

"TURN ONCE MORE," Daryl said, fastening a final piece of tape in place. "There. That should do it."

Taking a step back, Chelsea glanced from Daryl to Ramón. "What do you think?"

"I need to get back to my soufflé," Ramón said.

"I think I'm falling in love," Daryl said.

Chelsea stared at him. "Don't be ridiculous. You can't."

"Not with you, sweetie. It's this fabric. It's quite unique. It looks black at first, but there's a thread running through it that reflects the light." He rubbed the material between his fingers.

Chelsea heard someone draw in a deep breath. Raising her eyes, she saw that Pierre, the maître d', had raised his hand to his chest as if he'd just taken a blow. He was still staring at her with a bemused expression on his face. "Miss, I..."

Just then, she felt Daryl lift her skirt again. Glancing down, she saw that his head had disappeared beneath it.

"Daryl! What are you doing?"

"I have to know what material this is." Daryl's voice was muffled. "There has to be a tag somewhere with care instructions."

"Enemy approaching at one o'clock," Ramón announced.

Chelsea glanced up to see that Pierre was still staring at her. Beyond him, the scowling man was doing more than stare. He was striding across the bar toward them.

Quickly, she reached out and grabbed her coat from the stool. "Get up, Daryl. I don't want to get you and Ramón in trouble."

Daryl pulled his head out from beneath her skirt and made a quick assessment of the situation. "I think I'll stay right here. It's harder to hit a man when he's already on his knees."

Daryl had it right. The tall stranger certainly looked as if he wanted to hit someone. Quickly, she tried to shrug into her coat.

"Are you crazy?" Daryl said under his breath. "Don't cover up that skirt."

"What do you mean?" Chelsea asked.

"Take a look at Pierre. He's clearly smitten. Let's hope it works its spell on the white knight who is riding to your rescue." Picking up the edge of the skirt, Daryl waved it in the approaching stranger's direction.

"Stop that," Chelsea hissed.

When Daryl didn't drop her skirt, the man said, "The lady asked you to stop that."

2

CHELSEA FELT the soft brush of the skirt against her leg as Daryl released it, but the rest of her attention was totally focused on the man who stood three feet away. Though she was aware of the rugged good looks—the dark hair that grew past his collar and the nearly faded scar on his chin—her eyes never once left his.

They were the dark blue color of sapphires and right now there was a look in them that spelled *danger*. Beneath the sleek lines of that designer suit, this was a man poised for a fight.

The other men sensed it, too. Daryl shifted on his knees, Ramón swung around the end of the bar and Pierre cleared his throat. "Sir..."

"Come here."

Chelsea took a step forward, responding to the command in the stranger's voice before the words even fully registered in her mind. Immediately, a nightmare began to unfold before her. Rising to his feet in one smooth movement, Daryl assumed an attack stance.

"Back off, buddy," Ramón said, springing from one foot to the other just the way he did when he was working out in the boxing ring at the gym. "The lady's with us."

"Guys," Chelsea began. Not one of them so much as glanced her way.

"I don't like to see women fondled in public," the man said. "She's coming with me."

"Wrong," Daryl said, shifting his weight to his back foot. Chelsea recognized the move instantly. She'd seen Daryl practice it often enough in the living room of their apartment. The chivalrous stranger was about to have a foot planted smack in his chest—unless Ramón's right cross flattened him first.

"Stop!" Quite aware that she was trapped in a bubble of testosterone about to explode, Chelsea threw herself in front of the stranger and faced the three other men. "Stop it right now."

"Get out of the way, Chels," Ramón said.

"This will only take a second," Daryl assured her.

As they both moved forward, she threw her arms out to the side and took a quick step back into a rock solid chest. It occurred to her briefly that she might have chosen to defend the wrong person.

"I've got it, Daryl," Ramón said, bouncing closer. "I can still get one in over her head."

Suddenly furious, Chelsea drew herself up to her full height and fisted her hands on her hips. "What are you thinking? You can't cause a scene. Do you want to lose your jobs?"

It was the four-letter word—jobs—that caught their attention. Ramón stopped bouncing from foot to foot and something in Daryl's eyes flickered. Pierre gasped and began to wring his hands.

Pressing her advantage, Chelsea continued, "Ramón, you have a soufflé waiting for you. Daryl, your bar's unattended. Pierre, there's a line of people waiting to be seated." She held her breath then and waited.

Daryl was the first to slip out of attack mode. "You going to be all right, sweetie?"

"A lot better than if you had started a barroom brawl!"

He flicked a glance over her head at the man behind her, then turned and hurried back to his workstation. Ramón and Pierre quickly followed suit.

Chelsea waited, hoping that her would-be rescuer would leave also. But as she counted off five seconds, he remained right where he was, close, his body nearly brushing against hers. Her skin prickled from the proximity and she couldn't recall ever being so aware of anyone before. Drawing in a deep breath, she took a careful step away and turned to face him.

His eyes were even bluer than she had realized, his gaze more intense. For a moment, she felt her mind go completely blank. All she knew was the heat of his gaze as it moved from her eyes to her mouth and back. The only thought she could latch onto was that she was trapped in another bubble, only it wasn't testosterone this time. It was something hotter and much more dangerous.

Licking her lips, she discovered that they were warm, almost as if she were running a fever. She would have taken another step back, but she wasn't sure her legs would work.

"Daryl—is he your lover?"

Chelsea blinked. "*Daryl*? No...I mean...that's none of your business."

His brows lifted. "I nearly started a barroom brawl because he was poking his head and his hands up your skirt. I think I have a right to be curious."

She frowned. "He was just shortening it. My skirt, I mean. He's my..." she searched for a word, "dresser."

"I see."

"I believe your friend is waiting for you...at your table."

His lips twitched, and she watched his eyes lighten. She didn't think of sapphires this time, but of the clear blue of the sea on a hot summer day.

"I was wondering when you'd get around to dismissing me the way you did the others. You've had some experience defusing fights, I take it?"

"Three brothers," she said. Staring into those eyes for any length of time made it difficult to concentrate. Drawing in a deep breath, she narrowed her eyes and focused. "But I haven't been very successful in dismissing you."

This time his lips curved in a smile. "Perhaps because I don't have a sister to boss me around. Why don't we try this?" He took her arm and retrieved her coat from the floor where she'd dropped it trying to stop the fight.

"What are you doing?" she asked as he drew her up the stairs.

"I'm letting you get me out of the bar."

She shot him a glance. "You don't have to hold on to me. I can walk by myself."

He dropped his hand immediately and studied her for a minute. His eyes had gone very intense again and the smile faded from his face. "I want to ask you to have lunch with me."

"I can't. I'm on my way to an appointment. If you'll just give me my coat." Without another word of protest, he helped her into it. Chelsea told herself it was relief she was feeling, certainly not disappointment. Then his hand was beneath her arm, guiding her through the group of men in suits who were waiting for Pierre to seat them and out onto the sidewalk.

"Thanks," she said. Scanning the street for a taxi and not immediately spotting one, she risked looking at him again. "Thanks for..." In daylight, his eyes reminded her of the blue of the ocean at its deepest—fascinating, tempting.

"At least give me your phone number."

She blinked. "My phone number?"

"I'd like to see you again."

She blinked again as it suddenly struck her. The man had nearly gotten into a fight over her and then he'd invited her to lunch. Now he was asking for her phone number. Could the skirt actually be working? She beamed a smile at him. "That's great!"

Slipping a hand into his pocket, he drew out a small notebook and a pen. "What's your number?"

"Oh, I didn't mean...I mean I can't give you my

phone number. I just meant that it's great that you asked."

His gaze narrowed. "Then why can't you give it to me?"

"Lots of reasons," she said, stifling a sigh of relief—certainly not regret—as a taxi pulled up to the curb. "My roommates and I made this pact not to date, for one thing. And then there's this skirt."

"A skirt?"

"It's a long story, much too long to go into right now. You wouldn't believe it anyway. I didn't myself until just a few minutes ago." Pausing to get a breath, she frowned. "And it might be a fluke, but you have to admit that something happened in there. Which means it's much better for both of us if we never see each other again. Believe me." With the skill of a New Yorker, she scooted behind the man alighting from the taxi and slid into the seat.

"Wait," he said as she pulled the door shut.

As soon as the taxi lurched away from the curb, she looked back to see that he was scribbling something down in his notebook. The license plate of the taxi? Was he going to try to trace her that way? As she felt a wave of excitement wash over her, she told herself that it was because the skirt was evidently working! But she kept looking back until the taxi finally swerved around a corner to speed uptown.

AT TWO-THIRTY, Zach stood behind the desk in his father's office staring out the window. The tinted glass

offered a gloomy view of Rockefeller Center complete
with its landmark Christmas tree. Thunder grumbled
overhead and gray-as-soot rain pounded against the
pane.

It was a good thing that he didn't believe in omens,
Zach thought, because in a matter of a few hours the
day had turned as dark as the faces of the editorial staff
who'd streamed out of the conference room a few
minutes earlier. The meeting had taken less time than
he'd anticipated and not even his Aunt Miranda had
seemed enthused about the specifics of the plans he'd
unveiled for *Metropolitan* magazine.

The *real* meeting was taking place now. As he'd followed the staff members out of the conference room,
they'd managed to corner his aunt and drag her into
one of the nearby offices—for a private venting party,
he supposed.

Frowning, Zach shoved his hands into his pockets.
What exactly had he expected? None of the editorial
staff had seen him in years. It was ridiculous to suppose that they might trust him on sight. The last time
he'd visited his father's office, he'd been twelve.

No. Turning, from the window, Zach's frown deepened as he glanced around the room. This wasn't his
father's office anymore. It was his. How could he expect his employees to accept that until he did?

Moving toward the desk, he gripped the back of the
leather chair. His glance fell immediately on the small
ceramic Christmas tree sitting on one of its corners. His
first impulse had been to remove it. He didn't like re-

minders of the season. But he recalled the day he and his mother had brought the small tree to the office. He'd been five and his mother had let him sit at the desk while they waited for his father to join them. His gaze shifted to the gold-plated pen, still in its stand. He ran his finger over the engraved inscription. It had been a gift to his father from the president of the United States.

He'd been using the pen to draw pictures when his father had walked in. What Zach remembered most clearly about the incident was not his father's anger. His childhood had been littered with occurrences when he'd failed to behave the way a McDaniels should and his father had lashed out at him. No, what he recalled most about that fateful day were the tears his father's lecture had brought to his mother's eyes. She'd taken him skating at Rockefeller Center right after they'd left the office. It had just been the two of them and it was the last memory he had of his mother.

Pushing away from the chair, Zach turned back to the window. He rarely let himself think of his mother, yet it was the second time today that she'd popped into his mind. Earlier, he'd been reminded of her when the taxi with that woman in it had pulled away from the restaurant. For a moment, he'd thought of another taxi, one that had taken his mother away to the hospital that fateful day while he'd stood helplessly watching from the curb.

Ridiculous, he thought as he firmly pushed the image away. The childhood nightmare hadn't plagued him in years. And he hadn't been helpless this time. He'd copied down the license plate of the departing taxi.

Pulling his notebook and pen out of his pocket, he flipped it open and looked down at the numbers. If he hired a P.I., he could find out exactly where his mystery woman had gone. All he had to do was make a phone call. If he couldn't trace her that way, he'd have the investigator approach her *dresser* and her other champion in the chef's hat. One way or the other, he could see her again—if he wanted to.

He'd be much better off worrying about the fact that he did want to see her again than about some childhood memories that were much better off forgotten.

What exactly had gotten into him at the restaurant? That was the question his aunt had asked him the moment he'd returned to the table. He hadn't had an answer for her. He could hardly believe he'd nearly gotten into a fight in a public place over a woman he'd never met before. He rarely acted on impulse.

Indeed, he prided himself on thinking things through, weighing all the pluses and minuses before he acted. But he'd had an overpowering urge to protect that woman in the bar. Then he'd acted on impulse again when he'd asked her to join him for lunch.

He didn't know anything about her, only that she was different from the type of woman he was usually drawn to. He'd always been able to read them, predict what they would do. Not one of them would have thrown herself between three men who were about to start throwing blows!

His frown deepened. She needed a keeper. And that was just the kind of woman he always avoided. Still, he'd found her almost...irresistible.

Moving back to the desk, Zach frowned down at the license number. In his head, he could list all the minuses of getting in touch with her. He couldn't afford the time for any kind of relationship right now, not when his dream was within reach. It was his body that was giving him problems. His body wanted to see her again.

Hell, he wanted *her*. He had from the moment he'd walked down the steps into that bar and gotten a good look at her. And he didn't even know her name—yet. His frown deepened as the significance of the *yet* sank in.

"Well, you certainly are lost in thought."

Zach glanced up to find his aunt Miranda facing him across his desk.

"I knocked, but you didn't answer," she said studying him. "Are you all right?"

Smiling, he closed his notebook and tucked it back into his pocket. "I should be asking you that. You're the one they attacked after the meeting."

"They're upset," she said. "Change has that effect on people."

"And you're upset too, aren't you?"

"Me? Whatever gave you that idea?"

"You looked as if you were in pain during the meeting."

Miranda waved a hand. "That was because of my feet." Sinking into a chair, she stretched her legs out in front of her. "I should have insisted we take a taxi from the restaurant. These boots were definitely *not* made for walking!"

"You're avoiding a direct answer. Were you upset by some of the plans I unveiled for the magazine?"

Miranda raised her perfectly arched brows. "First I'm cross-examined by your staff and now you."

"Answer the question."

"And to think that I was the one who encouraged you to go to law school."

This time Zach said nothing. He merely waited.

"I still say you would have made a much better attorney than your brother if you'd decided to practice law. I would have loved to have seen you in a courtroom."

"You're stalling, Aunt Miranda."

She sighed. "I wasn't upset, merely surprised that you're making so many changes all at once."

Zach's eyes narrowed. "You don't think I'm nuts to want to change the focus of the magazine to include other cities besides New York?" That had been a big problem for some of the editors at his meeting.

Miranda shook her head. "Not at all. It's bound to increase your subscription numbers because it will appeal to more readers."

"Then what is it that you're tap dancing around? I'd

rather you came right out with it. You didn't seem to object to my idea to change the tone of the magazine and to attract a more intellectual audience."

"Good heavens, no. I'm all for a magazine that makes me think. It's your father who wouldn't have approved of that. He'd have told you that if you appeal to the eggheads, you'll be slashing your sales by fifty percent."

Zach studied her. "But you're not saying that."

"Not at all. I told you at lunch. *Metropolitan* has been in trouble for the past two years, even before your father became ill. Some changes are essential and I think that if anyone can turn it around, you can."

"*But?*"

Miranda wrinkled her nose at him. "There's no *but*. Really. I'm just a little concerned that Bill Anderson will turn in his resignation. He has a very short fuse, and he has a lot of influence over the rest of the staff."

"How many others will follow suit?"

Miranda thought for a moment. "Hal Davidson will send out his résumé and make sure he has a firm offer before he leaves. And Carleton Bushnell is so grumpy all of the time, it's hard to read him."

Bill Anderson had been covering the New York sports scene for almost twenty years while Hal Davidson's field had been politics. He'd rather not have to replace them, but it could be done. "What about Esme Sinclair?" Zach asked. A rather tall woman who dressed like a fashion plate and wore her steel gray hair pulled back tightly into a ballerina's bun. Esme had always intimidated him. She reminded him of the strict housemistresses he'd run up against in the boarding schools he'd been sent to.

"She'll stay. She's been with the magazine almost from the beginning. I think your father relied on her quite a bit."

"But I'm planning to eliminate the fashion and gossip stuff," Zach pointed out.

"That's the kind of *stuff* I frequently pick up a magazine to read," Miranda said and then quickly slapped a well-manicured hand over her mouth. "Sorry! Forget I said that. I promised myself I wouldn't."

Zach studied her for a moment. "That's the *but* you wouldn't talk about earlier, isn't it?"

Miranda sighed again. "I wasn't going to say it—but women do read a lot of magazines. And Esme has printed a couple of articles lately that have not only been highly amusing, but they've increased newsstand sales."

Zach's eyes narrowed. "I'm surprised that you approve of them. 'What Makes a Man a Hottie?'"

"Did you read it?"

"No. And I didn't read 'How to Hook a Hottie' either. Selling sexual innuendo is definitely not the way I want to go with the magazine. I can't imagine what Esme was thinking. I was rather hoping that she would consider retiring."

"Esme's been running the magazine since your father's illness. It's only been under her watch that the sales figures have picked up a bit."

Zach frowned. He hadn't known that. "I thought you were the one who had taken over for Father."

"Me?" Miranda pressed the palm of her hand against her chest. "I've never put in an honest day's work in my life."

Zach shook his head. "You've been on the board of McDaniels Inc., since it was founded."

"A figurehead position."

Zach knew better. He also knew that it was usually a waste of time to argue with his aunt. "I suppose your various charitable organizations run themselves?"

"They're run by people I've handpicked to do the job. That way I never have to lift a finger." Rising, Miranda took a tentative step toward him and winced. "Now that I've handpicked you to save *Metropolitan* magazine from collapse, I can go back to my apartment and get out of these killer boots. What we women endure for our vanity."

"I'll never be able to thank you for trusting me, Aunt Miranda," Zach said as he moved around his desk to put his arms around her.

"As far as thanking me goes, I'll expect to see you at the Christmas ball I'm hosting next Saturday." When he started to say something, she took his hands in hers. "I know that you don't like to celebrate the season, but I have a feeling your Mom would want you to."

"Aunt Miranda—"

"I've reserved two places at my table. Bring a guest."

Zach's brows shot up. "That sounds like an order?"

"It is. I know someone who'd be very happy to go with you," Miranda said.

Zach raised his hands, palms out in surrender. "I'll come to the ball. But no date. Aren't you ever going to give up trying to match me up with my soul mate?"

"Never."

"She doesn't exist."

Miranda tapped a finger against his chest. "You just haven't found her yet. When you do, you'll never let her go."

"No date, Aunt Miranda."

"Fine." Miranda sighed, a small pout replacing the smile on her face. "You won't find yourself a date. You'll come by yourself and you'll be too bored to stay once the dancing starts."

Zach grinned at his aunt as he took her arm and led her to the door. "I'll be bored from the moment they serve the appetizer and I'll be catatonic by the time the last course is removed. However, I will be there." When he opened the door, he found himself facing Esme Sinclair.

"I'd like a moment of your time, if I'm not interrupting," Esme said.

"You're only interrupting my failed attempt to persuade my nephew to let me find him a date for my Christmas ball. I'll get right out of your way."

It was with a certain amount of envy that Zach watched his aunt wave a hand and walk quickly toward the open door of an elevator. He found himself stifling an annoying impulse to bolt. He wasn't a child anymore and Esme Sinclair wasn't an old housemistress. Ushering her into the room, he closed the door, then moved to stand behind his desk.

Esme reached for the switch on the ceramic Christmas tree.

"I'd prefer that you didn't turn it on," Zach said.

Her hand stilled, then dropped to her side. "Sorry."

"What can I do for you, Ms. Sinclair?" Zach asked.

"Not a thing. I'm going to do something for you. I know that you want to immediately eliminate what you termed the fluffy sections of the magazine, but I'm afraid that won't be possible, at least for the next three issues."

Zach's eyebrows rose. "Why not?"

"I have a young lady in my office who's written two very fine articles for us recently. I bought them in an attempt to expand our audience among younger readers and the sales figures have gone up accordingly. This morning, before I was informed of your appointment, I had her sign a contract to provide us with three more articles. Her proposal is right here and I've also included copies of her other articles. I think they all fit into the fluff category." Handing him a folder, she continued, "The legal department says our best bet is to honor the contract."

"Or offer to buy it back," Zach said as he opened the folder. He recognized the name on the contract immediately. Chelsea Brockway was the writer he'd just been discussing with his aunt—the one whose articles on "hotties" were selling magazines. The last thing he wanted was to print any more of her work. He glanced up at Esme. "Why don't you arrange for me to speak with her?"

"I called her right after our staff meeting. She's waiting outside," she said as she moved toward the door.

It was the legs that Zach recognized first when the woman stepped into his office. Backlit by the lights from the hall, he could have sworn that they went right up to her waist.

3

"CHELSEA BROCKWAY, I'd like you to meet Zach Mc-Daniels, the new editor-in-chief at *Metropolitan*," Esme said as she drew Chelsea into the office.

Chelsea took two steps into the room, then froze the moment she recognized the man behind the desk. "You..." she glanced back at Esme, "this is Mr. Mc-Daniels?"

"In the flesh." Brows lifted, Esme glanced from Chelsea to Zach. "You two have met, I take it?"

"Not formally," Chelsea said. "We sort of ran into each other in a bar this morning."

"Oh?" Esme said.

"I was on my way here to sign my contract when he...Mr. McDaniels interrupted a conversation I was having with my...roommates. It was about... Well, I suppose that's neither here nor there, but we didn't know we would be meeting again. We didn't exchange names...or anything else." *Like phone numbers.* Chelsea made herself stop and take a breath. She was babbling. Nerves made her do that, and they'd invaded her stomach the moment that she'd recognized Zach McDaniels. The dive-bombing butterflies she could deal with. It was the simple rush of pleasure that disturbed her. She could still feel it tingling through her right down to her toes.

Hadn't she told herself that she never wanted to see him again? By the time she'd arrived at the McDaniels Building, she'd almost convinced herself. In the past two hours she hadn't thought about him more than four or five times, tops. Okay maybe six times at the very most. She certainly hadn't regretted not giving him her phone number, not even for a second.

"Won't you sit down?" Zach gestured to one of the chairs in front of his desk.

Chelsea moved to it and carefully settled herself on the edge of the seat before she steeled herself to glance up at him. The eyes were just as intense as she'd recalled. Once again she felt just as aware of him as she had in the bar that morning. What she needed was one of those protective shields, she decided. The kind that always protected spaceships from attack in the movies—invisible, soundless and impermeable.

Esme cleared her throat. "Do you want me to tell Ms. Brockway about the problem we were discussing?"

Chelsea dragged her gaze away from Zach's. "Problem?"

"I'll tell her," Zach said. "If you would just give us a moment, Ms. Sinclair?"

"I'll wait outside."

For a moment after Esme left the room, neither of them spoke. But the word *problem* began to repeat itself like a little drumbeat in Chelsea's mind. It was keeping perfect pace with Zach's fingers, which were tapping on his desk. The fingers were long and lean and Chelsea found herself recalling just how they'd felt pressed against the inside of her upper arm when he'd grasped it to lead her out of the bar. She should have had her invisible protective shield up then, too.

Deliberately sliding her gaze away from his hands, she raised it to his face. He was frowning at her.

"What?" she asked.

"I understand that you signed a contract with Ms. Sinclair for three articles."

She frowned right back at him. "Is there a problem with the contract?"

"When Ms. Sinclair negotiated it, she wasn't aware that I was taking over as editor-in-chief of the magazine and she had no way of knowing that I intend to make rather sweeping changes. What I want to propose to you is that I—"

The intercom on his desk buzzed and he leaned toward it to press a button. "Ms. Parker, I'd like you to see that I'm not—"

The last word of his sentence was drowned out by an angry voice that poured into the room. "...that idiot that I want to see him right now and I don't care who's in his office! Never mind, I'll tell him myself."

The door sprung open and a tall man with gray hair and a thickening waist strode into the room and tossed a letter in Zach's direction. It bounced off his shoulder and fell to the surface of the desk.

"That's my resignation," the man said, his face

growing more flushed by the moment. "I'm sure it's what you wanted."

"I'm sorry you feel the need to resign," Zach said.

"Sorry? Oh, you're going to be even sorrier when you get the rest of the resignation letters in the interoffice mail. But I wanted to do more than drop you a letter. I wanted to tell you a few things to your face."

"Go right ahead," Zach said, keeping his tone very even. "Perhaps you'd let me know why you feel you have to leave the magazine."

"Why? You know damn well why. Don't try to deny it. I've covered New York sports teams for the past twenty years and you made it quite clear at that meeting that you won't be needing my expertise anymore." He snorted. "Or anyone else's either."

"I never said that."

"Not in so many words. But what exactly am I supposed to do when you start 'spotlighting' other cities? Sit around and twiddle my thumbs?" Pausing, he waved a hand. "But that's not the real reason I'm walking out. You want to know what it is?"

"Yes," Zach said.

"Because running this magazine is just a game to you. When your big plans fail, you'll just shut the whole thing down and go on to another career. I said as much to your aunt, but she wouldn't listen."

"From now on, I'd appreciate it if you'd bring your complaints directly to me. Leave my aunt out of it."

The man's chin jutted out. "Fine. I'll tell you just what I told her. If your father had wanted you to run this magazine, he would have left it to you outright. I told her she was a fool to turn it over to you."

Zach circled around the edge of his desk. "I don't take kindly to anyone who calls my aunt a fool."

"I call 'em like I see 'em."

Springing up from her chair, Chelsea stepped into the older man's path just as he was about to stride forward. "You don't want to do this."

"The hell I..." Stopping short, he glanced down at her. "Who are you?"

"Chelsea Brockway." She extended her hand.

Frowning, he studied her for a moment, his eyes moving from her head to her feet, then slowly back up again. Finally, he took the hand she offered.

"And you're...?" she asked.

"Bill Anderson. Former sports editor." His eyes narrowed. "Brockway. You wrote that article on 'What Makes a Man a...' what was it again?"

"A *hottie*," Chelsea said as she tried to extricate her hand, but Bill held onto it.

"That's right. A *hottie*. My wife and daughter read it." For the first time since he stormed into the room, his expression lightened. "They had to explain to me what a *hottie* was."

"Did they like the article?" Chelsea asked.

Bill nodded. "Told me I should read it and pick up some tips." Then he glanced over her shoulder at Zach. "You're wasting your time here. He's going to run this magazine right into the ground. If you want, I could put in a good word for you at several other places."

She smiled. "Thanks, but I've just signed a contract for three more articles and you know what they say about 'a bird in the hand...'" She let the sentence trail off and tugged on hers. When Bill didn't take the hint, she said, "Speaking of hands..."

"Look, I'm headed down to Flannery's to join the rest of the staff for a drink. Would you like to join us?"

"Sure. I'd love to."

Chelsea felt Zach stiffen behind her. "The lady would like her hand back."

She didn't have to turn to get a sense of the intensity in Zach McDaniels's eyes. She could feel the heat of his gaze boring into her back. Since her hand was still in Bill's, she could feel the temper begin to build again in the older man.

"Mr. Anderson, I'll be happy to join you and the rest of the staff just as soon as I can." Using her free hand, she grabbed the envelope that had fallen on the desk. "In the meantime, I think you ought to take a little time to reconsider your resignation. Talk it over with your wife and your daughter. You know, you should never make an important career decision while you're angry."

When Bill finally released her hand to take the letter, Chelsea stifled a small sigh of relief.

He glanced at the envelope and then back at her. "You think I should consider staying on?"

"Definitely."

"You believe his plan for the magazine will work?"

"I have the utmost confidence in him," she said without hesitation.

"All right." He nodded. "I'll think about it."

"And talk to your wife about it," she said.

He nodded again as he turned to walk to the door. Before he left, he glanced back at her. "You'll come down to Flannery's?"

"Sure," she said.

ZACH TIGHTENED his rein on his temper as he watched the annoying Bill Anderson disappear through his office door. If the man had kept Chelsea Brockway's hand in his one more second, it would have bubbled up in spite of his efforts. Just as it had that morning in the restaurant when that bartender had put his head up her skirt.

It couldn't be jealousy he was feeling, could it? He'd already reminded himself that she wasn't his type. And he hadn't been wrong about that, he thought as he studied her. She was standing at the front corner of his desk her face turned toward the door. She had none of the sophistication and polish that he usually found attractive in a woman. Her short blond hair looked as if she'd styled it by running her fingers through it. Her skin was paler than he recalled and the sprinkle of freckles that ran along the curve of her cheekbone told him that she wasn't even wearing makeup.

As far as the clothes went...he skimmed them swiftly with his gaze. They couldn't be called even remotely stylish. The most that could be said about the green sweater was that it matched the color of her eyes. Then there was the skirt. He frowned as his gaze skimmed it from her waist down the length of those legs. From the side, he could see that it fit rather too well, and the way it hung smoothly over her hip and clung to her leg made him wonder if she wore anything beneath it.

What exactly had that chump she called her *dresser* seen when he'd poked his head under it?

The thought had something hot boiling up in him all over again. This time he recognized it as jealousy. He didn't like it when another man touched her for the simple reason that he wanted to be the one doing the touching. Right now his fingers were itching to trace her cheekbone, and then the more stubborn line of her jaw and then...

Chelsea cleared her throat. "You mentioned a problem. What is it?"

"You." The word was out before Zach could stop it.

"Me? What did I do?"

He could hardly tell her that she made him feel jealous. Or that he wanted to touch her. Really touch her. If he wasn't careful that might just pop out of his mouth, too. Worse still, he might actually do it. Before the urge could become too powerful, Zach shoved his hands in his pockets and made himself sit on the edge of his desk. It was time that he solved the problem of Ms. Chelsea Brockway once and for all. "Why don't you take a seat?"

She did, folding her hands on her lap just where the edge of her skirt gave way to the smooth, white skin of her thigh. "Do you have some concerns about the skirt?"

Zach watched the article in question inch its way further up her leg as she moved forward in the chair. His throat went dry. "You could say that."

"Believe me, I had those same concerns. A skirt that attracts men? None of us really believed what my friend said about it in college. That it was some sort of a man magnet. But I thought it was a great idea for an article. 'Can a Lucky Skirt Help a Single Girl Attract a Man in Manhattan?' Then Ms. Sinclair offered me a contract for three articles. That's a lot of pressure. Just before you interrupted us in the bar, I was thinking, what if it doesn't work? Then Pierre offered me a table and you asked for my phone number. What more proof could you ask for?"

Frowning, Zach shifted his gaze to her face. Staring at her legs was not helping him follow her at all. "I'm sorry. Proof of what?"

"Proof that the skirt works," Chelsea said, beaming a smile at him. "Do you usually ask women you've only met once in a bar for their phone number?"

Zach's eyes narrowed. "I've been known to do that before."

Chelsea held up a hand. "Okay. Maybe that's not a good example. Let me rephrase the question. Have you ever almost gotten into a fight in a bar over a woman who was not your date, a woman you'd never met?"

"No. I haven't."

"There. I rest my case." Leaning back in the chair,

she placed her hands on the armrest and the skirt moved another inch up her thigh. "There's definitely something about this skirt. Now that I know that, I'm sure I can deliver three articles about my adventures wearing it and about the problems of being single in Manhattan."

"Let me get this straight. You're proposing to write about a man-magnet skirt?"

"Exactly."

"That's the most ridiculous thing I've ever heard. Why would anyone want to read about it?"

"Because people are lonely, especially single people, and they're looking for relationships."

"I'm single and I'm not looking for a relationship."

Chelsea waved a hand. "Neither am I. But most people are. And in a big city like Manhattan, it's hard to find one. The dating scene can be really brutal."

"And you think writing about a *skirt* can change that?"

"It can give people hope."

"That's ridiculous. Your skirt is perfectly ordinary."

"Then why can't you take your eyes off of it?"

She had a point. Quickly, he tore his gaze away and looked her directly in the eye. "Your proof is far from conclusive. I could argue that I'm looking at you, not the skirt. And I didn't almost get into a fight because you were wearing this particular skirt. I almost got into a fight because your *dresser* Daryl had his head up it."

Chelsea lifted the hem and rubbed it between her fingers. "Daryl was fascinated because of the material.

He designs clothes and he'd never seen anything like it before. Here, feel it." She lifted the hem and waited for him to take it between his fingers. The moment he did, he caught her scent, delicate...exotic. It made him think of islands with white, sandy beaches stretching out endlessly in the moonlight.

"Not that I'm surprised Daryl had never seen anything quite like it before. My friend Torrie bought it on some tiny little island that is really off the beaten track."

As she continued talking, Zach rubbed the thin, silky material between his thumb and forefinger and thought of lying on that sandy beach with Chelsea beneath him as the waves pounded.... He tried to push the image out of his mind, but he was finding it hard to concentrate while his fingers were only inches away from that pale, smooth skin.

Maybe it reminded him of an exotic flower that he'd come across in Maui—or in the rain forests of Puerto Rico. He was finding it very hard to concentrate with his fingers only inches away from that pale smooth skin....

You'll never let her go.

The instant the words drifted through his mind, Zach shook his head. Where in the world had his aunt's words come from? He shook his head again, but he couldn't seem to eliminate the scent.

"The material in this skirt is woven from the fibers of a special plant. Supposedly, because it's been kissed by moonlight it has a very powerful effect on men."

Zach dropped the hem of the skirt and this time when he shook his head, the scent grew fainter. He shifted his gaze to stare at Chelsea Brockway. "What the hell are you talking about? Are you claiming that this skirt has some kind of magical power."

"Not magic. No, I wouldn't go that far." Chelsea began to twist the ring on her finger. "You have to admit, it does seem to have a definite effect on men. Do I look like the kind of woman that Pierre would offer a table to when he's booked solid? And I'm certainly not the kind of woman you would ever ask for her phone number. Not that I wanted you to. I didn't."

Her chin lifted as she drew in a deep breath. "I know that my phone number isn't relevant to...or has anything to do with..." She waved a hand and her ring fell to the floor and rolled under the desk. Zach dropped to his knees at the same time that she did and his hand covered hers when she reached for the ring.

"I'm sorry. Whenever I get nervous, I start to babble. Just tell me to shut up."

"Shut up," Zach said as his gaze slid to her mouth. It was close, barely an inch away, and her lips were slightly parted. And moist. He only had to move to taste her. A warning bell sounded in some part of his mind. He was a man who preferred to look before he leapt, but from the moment he'd first seen her in that bar, he'd been thinking and wondering...

Just one taste. One, he told himself as he closed the distance and covered her mouth with his. Impossibly sweet was the first sensation that poured through him.

But beneath the initial rush of flavor was a tartness that beckoned to him to taste again. Still cautious, he drew back and watched her eyes open slowly. They were a dark, rich green—beckoning, bewitching. Desire twisted sharply as needs began to battle within him. He should never have kissed her. He was going to kiss her again.

Though she hadn't moved away, he settled his free hand at the back of her neck to hold her still as he once more took her mouth with his. This time beneath the tartness he tasted a hunger that matched his own.

As the heat of it swelled within him, he could have sworn that the carpet shifted beneath his knees. He knew that thunder rumbled its way through the concrete and glass behind him, just as certainly as he knew that one taste of Chelsea Brockway was never going to be enough.

ALL CHELSEA knew was the pressure of his mouth against hers. She should have pulled back at that first tentative brush of his lips. There was always a price to pay for throwing caution to the winds and this time she was sure it would be high. As he deepened the kiss and the flavors exploded on her tongue, thoughts swirled through her mind. This was what the forbidden fruit in the Garden of Eden must have tasted like. This was what Paradise was lost over. Sensations shot through her body until she was sure she would drown in them. She could feel the hard press of each one of those fingers against the back of her neck, the impossible heat of those lips and the flavors on his tongue, too many to separate. But she wanted the time to try. She needed to try and identify them so that she would remember....

As his fingers slid into her hair, she moved her hands to his shoulders, not to push him away, but to grab on and cling. Then he shifted his mouth to nip at her bottom lip and an arrow of pleasure shot through her, so sharp, that she began to tremble. When she felt him suddenly stiffen and start to draw away, she pressed her fingers into the muscles in his shoulder to urge him closer.

THE SHARP KNOCKING at the door penetrated Zach's mind only seconds before he heard someone clearing her throat. Dropping his hands to Chelsea's shoulders, he eased her away from him and helped her to her feet. Then he turned to find Esme Sinclair standing at the office door.

"I'm sorry to interrupt. I just wanted to know if the problem we talked about has been resolved?"

Zach felt the same way he had when he was five and he'd been caught doing something he shouldn't in his father's office. Shoving the uncomfortable wave of emotion aside, he dropped his hands to his sides and stepped back from Chelsea. "Not yet," he managed to say before he turned and circled to the back of his desk. Not only hadn't he solved it; the problem was growing bigger.

When Esme moved to leave, he waved her into the

room. "Come in. I think it will be better if you're here while I try to explain our position to Ms. Brockway." Stalling a moment, Zach opened the file that Esme had given him earlier. He would concentrate on the facts. "These articles on the...on that skirt, won't suit the new direction that I want to take the magazine in."

"Why not?"

He glanced up in surprise to see Chelsea frowning at him. Her eyes were clear and he couldn't see any trace of the passion that he'd been feeling, that he'd thought she was feeling, too. "As I explained to my staff this afternoon, I'm cutting all the fluff. From now on *Metropolitan* is going to expand its intellectual and cultural appeal in an attempt to increase its readership." He glanced down at the file. "Features on *hotties* and man-magnet skirts don't mesh with my goals."

"Well, they should. My first two articles sold copies of your magazine."

"I like to look at things in terms of pluses and minuses. On the plus side—"

"Why?"

Zach stared at her. "Why what?"

"Why do you like to look at things in terms of pluses and minuses?"

"Because it allows me to make intelligent and informed decisions." When she said nothing, he continued. "On the plus side, your articles have drawn in new readers. On the minus side, these are not the readers I want. In fact, if I continue to publish you, I have a good chance of turning away the very reader I want to attract."

"But your emphasis on including only highbrow, intellectual stuff in *Metropolitan* is going to turn my readers away. And they've actually been buying the magazine. Ms. Sinclair told me that newsstand sales have jumped over thirty percent since my first article."

Zach's eyes narrowed. He hadn't expected an argument from her, especially not an articulate and well-framed one. He decided to change tactics. "I'm willing to make you a very generous offer to buy your contract back."

Chelsea folded her arms in front of her. "No."

He raised his brows. "You haven't heard my offer."

"I don't want the money. What I want, what I need, is the exposure. I want my name out there so that readers can get to know it. That's the plus I'm after and you can't give me that with a check."

"You can take the money and sell the articles to another magazine. Get the exposure some place else."

Chelsea shook her head. "That's not a sure thing. Ms. Sinclair liked my writing and she was willing to take a chance on the skirt thing. I may not find another editor willing to take that kind of risk." She waved a hand at him. "You're certainly not."

Zach sat down on the edge of the desk and began to enjoy himself. He hadn't gone through three years of studying law without a love for argument. Chelsea Brockway was a surprisingly able opponent. "Look, the bottom line is I'm not going to publish your articles. Just how hard do you want to make this?"

Moving forward, she pressed her hands flat on the desk and leaned toward him. "I want to make it impossible. I signed that contract in good faith."

"I can find a loophole in it."

For a moment she merely looked at him. Anger lightened the shade of her eyes to the color of emeralds, the kind with hints of fire in their depths. But even as he saw the flame, she managed to bank it. Straightening, she said, "Neither one of us wants me to sue."

He nodded, almost disappointed that she was about to concede. "Correct. Litigation would only end in some kind of settlement. Name a fair figure and I'll write a check."

"Wait." She raised a hand. "Your position is that the articles are 'fluff,' that the skirt really doesn't have any effect on men. To borrow your word, the idea is ridiculous. Therefore, it doesn't make the intellectual or cultural cut to be included in your magazine, right?"

Zach studied her for a moment, then nodded. "That's one way of putting it."

She put her hands on his desk and leaned toward him again. For one second he caught that exotic scent again.

"Have you ever gambled, Mr. McDaniels?"

"Sure."

"How about a bet? If I can convince you that the skirt works, you'll print the first article. If I can't convince you, you can tear up the whole contract. I won't ask for a cent."

When Esme cleared her throat, they jumped apart and turned. Zach had completely forgotten that anyone else was in the room.

"I just wanted to mention that your first article is due on my desk tomorrow. You'll have to convince him pretty quick."

Turning back to Zach, Chelsea held out her hand. "No problem. You can follow me to Flannery's and we'll see what happens. Do we have a deal?"

Never bet when it looks like you can't lose. It was one of the many lessons Zach had learned the hard way at boarding school. But his hand seemed to grasp Chelsea's of its own accord. "We have a deal."

4

"I'D LIKE TO KNOW how you talked Bill Anderson out of handing in his resignation."

Chelsea shifted her glance to the slender, light-haired man who sat directly opposite her in the booth. Hal Davidson wrote a regular column on the political scene for *Metropolitan*. He had smooth features and a practiced smile that probably served him quite well in his work.

She smiled right back at him. "I didn't do anything except suggest that he might want to sleep on an important decision like that."

Hal shook his head. "Well, you must be very persuasive. Before he walked into McDaniels's office, he had everyone fired up to resign. When he came out, he'd completely changed his tune."

"You sound disappointed."

Hal shook his head. "No. Merely surprised."

"I also suggested he might want to discuss it with his wife and daughter." Chelsea glanced down to the end of the booth where Bill Anderson sat in a chair. In the short time since she'd arrived at Flannery's, she'd observed that the sports editor clearly had a lot of influence over the other staff. She'd barely had time to take in the wood-paneled room and the mahogany bar trimmed in brass before Bill had spotted her and waved her over to the booth to introduce her to everyone as Esme's protégée, the one who'd written the articles on hotties. Since then she'd been wedged between a staff photographer named Chuck and the entertainment editor, a rather formidable-looking man in his early sixties named Carleton Bushnell.

The discussion at the table was centered mostly on the new boss and two things were very clear. They'd been very loyal to his father even when the magazine had begun to lose readers, and they didn't trust Zach. Bill Anderson and Hal Davidson were his most vocal critics. Their reasons ranged from his being too young to the fact that at the age of thirty, he'd hopscotched through several careers. First he'd gone to law school, then instead of going into practice he'd moved all over the country writing freelance for several newspapers and magazines.

Letting the conversation hum around her, Chelsea looked around the bar. Flannery's was a six-block walk from the *Metropolitan* offices at Rockefeller Center, and it was nearly filled with what looked like an after-work crowd, mostly men and a few women in suits. Even the four men who spoke with definite Texas drawls at a nearby table struck her as business travelers rather than tourists. The scent of whiskey, beer and popcorn filled the air, and in a corner a jukebox played the blues.

Each time the heavy, beveled glass door was pushed

open, she glanced toward it, but so far Zach McDaniels hadn't arrived. The good news was he hadn't missed anything. The bad news was he hadn't missed anything. So far the skirt hadn't gotten much attention. Of course, it was a little difficult for it to have much of an effect on anyone when it was completely hidden by a table and the staff of *Metropolitan*.

"Bill said you have absolute faith in McDaniels."

The moment Chelsea realized Hal Davidson was talking to her, she dragged her gaze from the door back to him.

"You've known him for a while, I take it?"

"Well," Chelsea paused when she realized that everyone in the booth was looking at her. She couldn't very well tell them that she'd told Bill that on the spur of the moment to defuse a fight. "Not that long. But he seems to be a man who knows how to get what he wants."

"Yeah, but what he wants could easily sink this magazine," Hal pointed out.

"If you think he's wrong, why don't you tell him so?" Chelsea asked.

Hal reached for his glass, the ring on his pinky catching the light. "Are you going to be doing any more articles?"

"Three more, I hope."

Hal stared at her in surprise. "Not in the same vein as your last one, I'll bet."

"Actually, I'm writing about my adventures when I wear this skirt one of my college roommates gave me."

Pausing, she leaned forward and pitched her voice lower. "It's supposed to attract men."

"You're kidding," Carleton Bushell said, turning to her. "You can't think a piece of clothing possesses special powers."

"Who knows?" Chelsea said. "Don't all of you have something that you think brings you luck—like a special tie that you always wear to an interview?"

Carleton narrowed his eyes and she noticed that once more all of the men at the table were looking at her. Some of their expressions were skeptical; others were thoughtful. Bill Anderson was the one who finally spoke. "I have a special hat I always wear when I go fishing."

"There you go." Glancing around the table, she decided to push her advantage. "Think about your wives and girlfriends. Don't they have something that they wear that you like a whole lot, something that sort of gives off a signal?"

Carleton Bushnell chuckled. "Well, if young McDaniels is going to print an article like that, maybe the shift he's making in the magazine won't be as drastic as he outlined this afternoon."

"Well, I'm—" Chelsea began, intending to tell them that she was still trying to convince Zach to publish the articles, but Carleton Bushnell had turned to Bill Anderson.

"I think you were right to hold off on that letter of resignation. Perhaps we ought to tell the guy what we think and then cut him a little slack. We all know that some changes have to be made. The magazine's been losing subscribers ever since the old man got ill. Could be that a new direction is what we need."

"Yeah, but what direction? That's the question," Bill Anderson said.

"He's hardly going to increase sales numbers by turning *Metropolitan* into a literary magazine," Hal pointed out.

"Well, this young lady isn't exactly writing literature, and young McDaniels is buying her articles." Carleton winked at Chelsea. "You got any tips for someone my age."

Bill let out a whoop of laughter. "There isn't a fire hot enough to heat you up, Bushnell."

Since he was old enough to be her father, Chelsea winked at Carleton. It was her chance to get out of the booth. "Ask me to dance and I'll share a few secrets."

"Whoa," the photographer said. "He's a dangerous man, Ms. Brockway. You'd be safer dancing with me."

"Safe?" Carleton's crack of laughter filled the air. "The lady doesn't want safe. You're either a *hottie* or you're not," he said as he slid from the booth drawing Chelsea with him.

She was just stepping into his arms on the small square of parquet floor in front of the jukebox when she felt the chill of the door opening again. Chelsea knew instantly that Zach had entered the bar. She felt the pressure of his gaze on the back of her neck, a tightening in her stomach and a weakness in her legs.

Drawing in a deep breath, she managed not to sag

against Carleton. When he swung her around, she saw
Esme first and then her gaze locked with Zach's. For
one long moment there might have been no one else in
the room. Every sensation that had flooded her system
when he'd kissed her moved through her again—the
spiraling pleasure, the urgency, the incredible craving
for more. It had been too much. It hadn't been nearly
enough.

Carleton swung her around again, and she very
nearly lost her balance.

"Sorry," she said, glancing up at him.

"Some guys have all the luck."

"What?"

"I'm not too old to know when the woman I'm dancing with is looking at another man."

"If you mean... It's not what you're thinking," she
made the mistake of glancing at Zach again. He was
scowling. "I'm not. We're not..." She stumbled.

Carleton grinned at her. "Make sure you tell him
that when he comes over to pound his fist into my
face."

"Maybe I should go powder my nose."

"Much obliged. My nose owes you one."

Unfortunately, the rest rooms were located down a
corridor near the entrance to the bar and although she
kept her gaze averted, Chelsea was sure that she could
feel Zach's eyes on her every step of the way. She even
imagined that she could feel the pressure of his gaze as
it moved down the length of her body. That was ridiculous. Her legs were tingling because she'd been sit-

ting too long—or because she hadn't danced in a long time. But the feeling was still there even after she turned down the narrow hallway. Running the last few steps, she grabbed a door handle and pulled.

"Whoa, little lady." Huge hands gripped her arms from behind, lifting her off her feet and setting her down in the hallway. "I don't think you want to go in there."

Chelsea glanced at the stick figure of a man on the door she'd just opened. Then turning around, she faced her rescuer—one of the biggest men she'd ever seen.

"Thank you," she managed.

"No thank you is...neceshary." He hiccuped. "Pardon me." One huge hand patted his stomach. "In my part of the country, we enjoy rescuing pretty ladies."

Chelsea recognized him as one of the men with the Texas drawls she'd noticed earlier. "Thanks anyway."

"No problem. But aren't you forgetting shhomething?" He took a shuffling step forward, which she countered by taking a quick step back. His face was flushed and after one quick but thorough glance from the top of her head to her feet and back again, he looked as though he might like to swallow her whole.

"What?" she asked, watching him warily.

He hiccuped. "In Texas, one good turn deserves another. Even you Yankees must live by that rule."

"Sometimes." She tried to figure out a way past him. The man seemed harmless enough, but he literally blocked the entire width of the hallway.

"How about a...dance?"

"I'd love to, but I have to use the ladies' room. It's got to be the next one down."

He smiled at her as he stepped back into the wall and used one hand to wave her by. "Go right ahead, sugar. I'll be waiting for that dance."

She hurried past him and pulled open the door of the ladies' room.

"You're gonna love the Texas two-step, little lady."

Chelsea shut the door and leaned against it for a moment. She'd worry about Mr. Texas later. Right now she had to figure out what to do about Zach McDaniels.

What in the world was the matter with her, she thought as she walked toward the woman she saw reflected in the wall-to-wall vanity mirror. She had to get a grip. She'd been thinking so much about Zach McDaniels that she'd very nearly walked into the men's room.

She stared at her reflection in the mirror. "Focus."

She had to prove to Zach that the skirt worked. In her mind, she tried to picture herself doing the two-step with Mr. Texas. Would that do it? Then she tried to visualize herself sitting on one of those burgundy upholstered stools at the bar, her legs crossed, surrounded by men who were laughing at something she'd just said.

That would be better, but even as the image formed, her gaze dropped to her mouth and the memory of Zach's kiss flooded into her mind instead. Lifting her hand, she touched her fingers to her bottom lip. Never had anything stirred her that deeply, that intensely. And it had happened so fast. He'd pressed his mouth to hers and... Bam! Her response had been instantaneous. So...elemental. Nothing, no one had ever made her react like that before.

Narrowing her eyes, Chelsea studied her reflection more closely. There had to be an explanation. But she looked like the same old Chelsea. Her gaze and her thoughts both drifted lower to the skirt.

No. It couldn't be. Zach McDaniels was not her true love. If the skirt was working any magic on him, she'd have to find a way to reverse it. He was all wrong for her. He didn't even want to publish her because her writing style didn't mesh with his new direction for the magazine.

Slowly, she met her own gaze in the mirror. He was exactly the kind of man her mother had warned her about. He was rich and charming—just the type who would walk away from her like her father had.

Hadn't he admitted he'd asked women in bars for their phone numbers before? He'd probably kissed women on the floor of his office before, too!

Hadn't her experience with Boyd the bum taught her anything? She'd been in New York less than a year when she'd fallen for a man who was only interested in a brief fling. She was not going to make that mistake again.

Pressing a hand against her stomach, she tried to push down the panic. She had to get a grip. She didn't really believe in the power of the skirt, did she? Narrowing her gaze, she stepped back from the mirror. It was just a plain, black skirt. Just a plain, black skirt. If she kept repeating that to herself, and if she worked fast enough, she could win her bet with Zach, write the articles and then never have to wear it again. She'd overnight it to Kate or Gwen. Then she'd be safe.

"Have you given up on winning your bet?"

Startled, Chelsea raised her eyes to see Esme Sinclair shutting the door to the ladies' room behind her.

"No," she said, smiling at the older woman. She hoped that when she reached Esme's age, she could look half as put together as the older woman did. Glancing back at her own image she decided it was a long shot.

"Zach sent me to check on you." Moving to the vanity counter, Esme pulled a lipstick out of her purse. "I think that was a foolish move you made back at the office."

Chelsea's eyes flew to Esme's in the mirror and she could feel the heat rise in her cheeks. "If you mean... I didn't. I mean...the kiss...wasn't what you think."

The woman's perfectly plucked brows rose slightly. "Actually, I was referring to how you convinced him to let you demonstrate how the skirt works. It would have been smarter to take his offer. He would have been very generous, I think."

"I wasn't thinking about the money."

"No. But perhaps you should." Esme touched up her lipstick, then slipped the tube back into her purse.

Chelsea ran her hand down the skirt with a frown. "You're probably right. Now, I'm stuck trying to figure out a way to make the skirt work." *But not work on Zach.*

"Tell you what. I'll make a few phone calls tomorrow and see if someone would be interested in your articles."

Chelsea turned to the older woman. "You've already done so much for me. How can I thank you?"

"You don't have to. I know what it is like to become a casualty of war in the publishing business."

"Thank you." Chelsea beamed a smile at her. "You've given me the courage to go back out there and learn the Texas two-step."

ZACH TOOK the glass the bartender handed him and pushed a bill across the top of the bar. Then he turned his attention back to the hallway Chelsea Brockway had disappeared into. He'd sent Esme to check on her five minutes ago. Taking a long swallow of his beer, he shifted his glance to the large Texan at a nearby table. It was the same man who'd followed Chelsea down that hallway and ever since he'd returned to his table, he'd been boasting loudly to his friends that a sexy little filly with emerald-green eyes had promised him a dance. Zach didn't doubt for a minute that the man was referring to Chelsea.

What was she going to do next? If he could just figure that out... What would he do then? Figure out a way to stop her?

Frowning, he took another swallow of his beer. Evidently she was prepared to go to any lengths to convince him that the skirt could attract men. He wondered how many others she'd wrapped herself around on that dance floor before he'd come in and seen her in Carleton Bushnell's arms. The man had been with *Metropolitan* as long as Zach could remember and he couldn't recall one instance when he'd seen the man smile. Miranda had referred to him quite accurately as a *grump*. But the old guy had actually been laughing when he'd been dancing with Chelsea and he was old enough to be her grandfather.

If betting with her had been a mistake, kissing her had been an even bigger one. Zach took another swallow of his beer. It wasn't just her taste that he couldn't get out of his mind. It was the feeling that had rushed through him. There was something about it—a mixture of the familiar and the totally unexpected that he found...*fascinating*.

He wanted to kiss her again. No, more than that, he wanted to walk down that hallway, find her and carry her off someplace—to a moonlit beach. He could almost smell the ocean, hear the waves crashing, feel them push forward and pull back, making the sand shift beneath them as he took her—

With a sudden start, Zach set his empty beer glass down on the bar. What in the world was the matter with him? He couldn't recall having that kind of primitive fantasy about any other woman.

"There she is!" The man from Texas erupted from his chair and waved his hand. "I'm right over here, sugar."

CHELSEA SMILED as she waved at Mr. Texas. "Wish me luck," she said in a low voice to Esme before she began to thread her way across the room. She was not going to look at Zach. That would be a mistake. A very big mistake, she decided as she met his eyes across the crowded bar. The moment she did, she couldn't seem to move anymore. Her body seemed trapped, paralyzed between two opposing signals from her brain. A part of her wanted to walk toward the Texan and win her bet. Another part wanted to walk toward Zach. Above the noise, above the bubble of panic rising within her, she heard music from the jukebox. The tune was old, the lyrics familiar—ones about finding your true love.

Could the skirt be tugging her toward Zach?

No! It was just a plain, black skirt. A plain, black skirt.

"Hey, little lady! Over here!"

Out of the corner of her eye she could see that Mr. Texas was plowing toward her.

The two men were both getting closer. She had to do something. But her feet might as well have been planted in concrete.

A large, firm hand closed around her arm. "That's our song they're playing."

Finally wrenching herself from Zach's gaze, she laid her hand on the Texan's broad chest and smiled up at him. "Yes, it is. All my life I've wanted to learn the two-step."

5

ZACH PUSHED another bill toward the bartender and handed the glass of white wine he received in exchange to Esme. He'd considered ordering another beer, but decided against it. He'd already had two and they hadn't solved the problem of what he was going to do about Chelsea Brockway.

His gaze moved back to the dance floor where she was still being bounced around the floor by the Texan. From what he could make out, the Texas two-step was just an excuse Texas men invented to be able to touch a woman on various parts of her body. Chelsea seemed to be enjoying herself. Turning back, he signaled the bartender for another beer.

What he wanted to do, what he'd nearly done when that overgrown cowboy had first started walking toward her was to grab her arm and drag her out of Flannery's. If he had, she could have claimed she'd won the bet. Or she could have refused to go with him. It was impossible to predict with her. His gaze shifted back to the dance floor in time to see her laugh at something the Texan said. How could she be enjoying herself?

"She's a clever and determined young lady," Esme said.

Zach turned to study the older woman at his side. "You think I ought to print her articles."

Esme met his eyes. "You're the new boss. You can do whatever you want. If someone had bothered to tell me that you were going to be the new editor-in-chief before I had Ms. Brockway sign that contract this morning, we both could have saved ourselves a lot of trouble."

"I asked that no one be told." Zach thought he saw something flicker in Esme's eyes, but before he could decide what it was, it was gone. "You're upset because my aunt turned the magazine over to me, aren't you?"

Taking a careful sip of her wine, Esme shifted her gaze to the dancers. "Not upset. Surprised. Your aunt Miranda and your father have always been full of surprises. I should have expected it."

But she hadn't, Zach realized. Had she expected that her job as temporary editor-in-chief would become permanent? He didn't much like the fact that getting his own dream caused someone else to lose theirs. "You wanted to run *Metropolitan* yourself, didn't you?"

Esme's eyes flew to his. "Me? If I had wanted to run a magazine, I should have left *Metropolitan* years ago."

"Why didn't you?" he asked.

"I was happy working for your father," Esme said.

Raised voices on the dance floor had Zach turning in time to see that one of the Texan's friends had joined him. Neither of the men looked happy and Chelsea stood between them. Zach quickly began to push his way toward them.

"It's my turn to dance with the little filly," the friend bellowed, pulling at Chelsea's arm.

"One more dance and you can have her," Chelsea's partner said, keeping a tight hold on her other arm.

The other man grinned. "Tell him you'd rather dance with me, little lady."

"I don't think the lady wants to dance with either one of you," Zach said as he reached them.

The two very tall Texans dropped Chelsea's arms and whirled to face him. The one who'd been dancing with her slapped his hand against his thigh as if expecting to find a six-gun.

"Thish little lady is goin' to dance with me...and then with my friend," he said.

"Yeah. Butt out," the other one added.

"Now, wait just a minute," Chelsea said, trying to wedge herself between them. "This isn't a shoot-out at high noon."

They ignored her as they moved in unison toward Zach.

Zach looked from one to the other as he rolled on the balls of his feet. Out of the corner of his eye, he saw that Carleton Bushnell and the other members of his staff had moved to the edge of the small dance floor.

"I'm taking the little lady out of here," Zach said.

"Where we come from, we don't take kindly to poachers," Chelsea's dance partner said. Of the two, he was bigger. But his friend looked meaner.

Keeping his eye on his opponents, Zach said, "Chelsea, move over by Bill."

"Not until you stop this—"

Out of the corner of his eye, Zach saw Bill Anderson take his cue and step forward to draw Chelsea away.

"Whoooopee," the meaner looking one shouted. "It looks like we got ourselves a fight!"

The bigger one hiccuped as he raised his fists. "He's mine."

But his friend stepped in front of him and threw the first punch.

Zach ducked to the right, then pivoted to bring the edge of his hand down hard on the side of the man's neck. The meaner-looking one fell like a rock.

There was a flurry of movement as Chelsea streaked forward and latched onto her dance partner's arm. "Stop it. Stop it, right now."

"Thish will only take a second, sugar," the man said, shrugging her off with the same ease that he'd been bouncing her around the dance floor. This time both Bill and Carleton stepped forward to draw her away.

Zach figured he had about two seconds to decide how to play it—not that he had a lot of options. The dance floor was small with people lined up three deep around it. His opponent had fists the size of small hams, and in spite of the fact that he'd had a lot of beer, he wasn't likely to make the same mistake that his friend on the floor had.

Dodging the first punch, Zach leaned to the side and aimed one quick kick to the man's midsection. The force sent the guy falling backward to land on his butt. A second later, he crumpled forward, clutching his stomach.

Turning, Zach found Bill Anderson at his side with Chelsea.

"You'd better get her out of here while they're still on the floor."

"Thanks." Taking Chelsea's arm, Zach drew her with him through the crowd. Carleton Bushnell and the others on his editorial staff had formed a human barricade to keep his path free of the other two Texans. One of them broke through it just as he pushed Chelsea through the beveled glass door.

"Hurry," he said. Outside, the rain had stopped, but there wasn't a taxi in sight. Keeping her hand in his, he said, "We're going to have to make a run for it."

And run they did. To the end of the street, around the corner and up another block. She kept up with him without a question or a complaint. When he glanced down at her, he could have sworn that she was enjoying herself. As they raced around the next corner, he was surprised to find that he was, too. He was almost disappointed when the big Christmas tree at Rockefeller Center came into view. Slowing to a walk, he glanced over his shoulder. "I don't think they followed us."

"Lucky for us, they left their horses in Texas. Otherwise, I'm sure they would have saddled up."

He was swallowing a laugh when he stopped and turned to her. "Are you all right?"

"I'm fine," she said, drawing in a deep breath. "But my skirt's a little the worse for wear."

He glanced at it and saw that half the hem was hanging about three inches longer than the rest. It also seemed to sag at her waist.

"I think the two-step did it in." Her eyes were brimming with amusement when they met his.

His laugh escaped at the same time hers did. But even after the laughter died, he didn't look away. He was too absorbed in watching her. It might have been the play of the light thrown by a streetlamp over her skin or it might have been her scent tangling his thoughts, but for the first time, he realized that she was beautiful. The desire he felt moving through him was primitive, elemental and almost irresistible.

You'll never let her go...

"You know, I've never been fought over in a bar before. And for it to happen twice, well, almost twice in one day..."

Struggling to gather his thoughts and follow what she was saying, Zach dropped his gaze to her lips.

"And you did so well—no fuss, a minimum of breakage."

It had been a mistake to look at her mouth because he wasn't reading her lips. Only half of his mind was following what she was saying. The other half was imagining what it would be like to taste her again. That kiss in his office should have taken care of it, but that one taste had merely increased his hunger.

"I'm babbling again when we really should be talking about business."

Zach tore his gaze away from her lips. "What?"

"The bet. Did I win it? Are you going to publish my articles?"

You'll never let her go...

"Yes." The word slipped out almost of its own accord. He was reaching for her when she threw her arms around him. For a moment her cheek was pressed against his. "Thank you so much."

When Zach wrapped his arms around her to draw her closer, she shivered. Immediately, he set her away and swept her with his gaze. "You're freezing. You don't even have a coat on." Quickly, he began to unbutton his jacket.

Chelsea took a quick step away. "Don't be silly. I'll be fine once I get in one of those taxis—" Pausing, she glanced around. "I really better get going. Ms. Sinclair wants that article on her desk by noon tomorrow."

"I think there's a stand over there past the skating rink and beyond the Christmas tree," Zach said.

As she started in that direction, Zach slipped his jacket around her shoulders and fell into step beside her.

They walked in silence for a few minutes. Chelsea racked her brain for something to talk about. But every time she breathed in, she could smell Zach's scent, and it seemed to be making her brain foggy. That wasn't the worst part. For a moment there when she'd hugged him, she hadn't wanted to let go. Pushing the thought out of her mind, she made herself take in her surroundings.

At seven, the skating rink was still crowded with tourists and native New Yorkers who weren't ready yet to run back to their tiny apartments. Music poured out of the speakers—a Christmas carol of course. Then there was the tree. Huge and rather gaudy.

"Did you ever notice that everywhere you turn, someone is shoving Christmas down your throat?"

Zach nearly stumbled on the steps they'd started to climb. It was the last thing he'd expected her to say. "I've noticed."

"But you don't mind because this is the most joyous season of the year, right?"

"No. As a matter of fact, the season is rarely joyous for me and I find all the reminders annoying." He couldn't recall anyone who'd ever understood that.

Chelsea stopped and turned to face him, pitching her voice really low. "You really don't like Christmas then?"

"Not particularly."

"Shhhhh," she warned him. "Say that too loud and someone will shout 'Bah! Humbug!' at you."

Zach grinned. "I've noticed that, too."

A quick, frigid slap of wind hit them. "See. We're being punished for actually confessing to not liking Christmas. If we're not careful, that monster of a Christmas tree might even fall on us."

With a laugh, Zach took her arm and urged her up the last of the steps.

"Of course, there are some pluses, you know. To being a Christmas hater, I mean."

"Do tell."

Chelsea's lips curved. "You don't get caught up in the commercial rat race and doing all the decorating and baking. I've always left that up to my roommates. How about you?"

"I don't have roommates."

"What's on your list of pluses? I'm sure you have some."

"No, I can't say that I have." Zach turned to her, suddenly curious. "What turned you off on the holiday? Did Santa disappoint you?"

"No, I always had lots of presents under the tree. It's no big deal really." They'd begun to walk again, circling around the huge Christmas tree. She'd never told anyone except her college roommates what had soured her on Christmas, but it seemed easy to tell Zach, perhaps because he wasn't enamored of the holiday either. "I enjoyed the whole season thoroughly until I was old enough to know that my father was living and never wanted to see me."

"Why not?" Zach asked.

"Mom says he just didn't want the responsibility. And it would have been different if I hadn't been born on Christmas Eve. When I was old enough to know that he never even came to the hospital to see me, it sort of cast a pall on the whole season for me. A bad memory can do that, don't you think?"

"Yes." When she glanced up at him, she saw that he

was looking past her—at some memory of his own? She was about to ask when he glanced back down at her. "You've never seen your father?"

She shook her head. "It was part of the deal my mother made. He paid for my college education. In return, I never contact him." She studied him for a moment. "Now you know my deepest darkest secret. How about telling me yours?"

He smiled, taking her arm and guiding her around the tree. "Another time. Right now, I'd rather know more of yours. Why do you want to write for magazines?"

"That's not much of a secret. My mother would tell you that I've always loved writing, creating images and ideas with words. Magazines seemed an easier goal than a book. One of the pluses is that you can write shorter pieces and get published faster than if you write books."

"Not faster than if you wrote for a newspaper," Zach pointed out.

"No, but you get a longer shelf life. Another definite plus. How about you? Why do you want to run a magazine?"

"It's always been my dream. When I was little, it was probably because it was what my father did. Later, I decided that it was a way to establish a forum for people to exchange ideas. It's an opportunity to make a real difference in the world."

He spoke with passion about his work. She could see it in his eyes, hear it in his voice. She couldn't help but admire him for it. "I can see why you look down your nose at my articles. But don't you think there's more to life than ideas?"

He shot her a sidewise glance. "*Hotties* and man-magnet skirts, for instance?"

She shook her head. "Not just that. I was thinking about all the things that people do just to relax with one another and have fun—movies, museums, skating, that kind of thing. For my second article on the skirt, I'm going to wear it to the Museum of Modern Art and I'm going to go skating in it right here in Rockefeller Center."

They'd reached the street, and across it, two taxis waited at a stand. Zach grabbed her arm as she stepped off the curb, then turned her to face him. "I don't like the idea of you wearing that skirt around alone. It seems to attract...trouble."

"That's the whole point," Chelsea said. "Otherwise, there wouldn't be anything to write about."

For a moment, Zach ran the idea over in his mind. He would have preferred to have more time to weigh the pluses and the minuses.

"I don't want the magazine to be responsible for anything hurting you," he said with a frown.

Her brows shot up in surprise. "If you're worried that I'll sue, I won't."

She was halfway across the street before he caught her arm again. "I've got a better idea. My aunt is throwing a Christmas ball for charity next Saturday night. Why don't you come with me?"

Chelsea glanced up at him, a frown slowly forming on her forehead. "No, I'm sorry, but I can't. I don't date."

Zach stared at her as several emotions ran through him. Surprise, he could understand. She should have said yes. Any other woman would have said yes. But he was *not* disappointed. "Why not?"

"I told you before, it's a pact I made with my roommates. Dating is too hard. Physically, it takes too much effort to get out there and meet people. And emotionally, it can be really distracting, not to mention devastating. So we've sworn not to date until we get our careers more established. And right now, my priority has to be the articles."

Zach studied her in the moonlight that had begun to stream through a break in the clouds.

You'll never let her go...

"Don't think of it as a date. It's an opportunity to try out that skirt of yours at my aunt's ball. Most of Manhattan society will be there. Think of the article you can write. It will be much safer than going to the Museum of Modern Art or coming here to skate."

He could almost hear the wheels turning in her head.

"I'm offering you a business opportunity."

Hesitating, she began to twist her ring again. "As long as we're clear that it's not a date."

Zach managed to keep his expression absolutely neutral. "Crystal clear."

Later, he wasn't sure what alerted him to the danger—a gleam of moonlight off chrome or the sudden sound of an engine as it accelerated. But the car had appeared out of nowhere and it was close, bearing down on them fast.

Gripping her tightly to him, Zach tried to get out of its path. The car had momentum going for it. He didn't, and Chelsea's weight was slowing him down. The opposite curb seemed too far, the roar of the engine too close. Vehicles, parked bumper to bumper, blocked his path. At the last second, he lifted Chelsea and vaulted with her onto the hood of a car. Twisting, he took the brunt of the impact, then holding her tightly, he rolled.

Metal screamed against metal. Sparks flew. Zach registered that much before he dragged her with him to the sidewalk. He was on his feet in a second, still holding Chelsea close. Up the street, the dark blue sedan ran the red light, too far away for him to make out the plate.

For a second, he didn't move. There were too many emotions pounding through him. Fear. The coppery taste of it seared the back of his throat. He hadn't thought they were going to make it. He tightened his arms around Chelsea. "Are you all right?"

He felt her nod against his chest. Slowly, he moved his hand up her back and settled it at the nape of her neck. He could feel how slender she was, how fragile and he almost hadn't been fast enough. Fury bubbled up, hot and potent as lava, and he struggled to contain it. "Are you sure you're all right?"

"Pretty sure." Her voice was muffled. "I'm having a little trouble breathing."

Easing her gently away from him, he watched carefully as she shrugged her shoulders, bent her arms and shook her legs, one at a time. His own adrenaline was fading and he was becoming all too aware of the pain singing through his shoulder. His knees felt like jelly.

"Everything's fine, except for my feet. The effects of that Texas two-step are setting in." Her voice was light, but her eyes when they met his still held traces of fear. "That was close."

"Too close." Zach reached for her and held her. Let her hold him. As the seconds ticked by, he drew in a deep breath and let it out. Even as it left his body, he could feel the fear and the fury begin to pour out of him. He felt the thudding of her heart begin to slow. He'd wanted to hold her. Only moments ago, he'd imagined what it would be like to have her in his arms again, but this was different. It was nothing like the other time in his office. There was no heat, no searing spiral of desire. Instead, there was warmth, sweet and...surprising.

Chelsea was the one who drew back. "Thank you."

"For what?"

"Rescuing me from a drunk cowboy, saving my life, asking me to your aunt Miranda's Christmas ball, honoring my contract with *Metropolitan* and...let me see...offering me your coat." She paused to draw in a breath. "Did I forget anything?"

For some reason he couldn't explain, Zach suddenly felt like laughing. "Can I get back to you on that?"

"Sure," Chelsea said.

Throwing an arm across her shoulder, he drew her toward the waiting line of taxis up the street. "In the meantime, you can thank me for seeing you home before you catch pneumonia."

"Thank you."

They were both laughing as he opened the door of the cab.

"IT SOUNDS like a date to me. Doesn't it sound like a date to you, Ramón?" Daryl asked as he added steaming water to the pan that Chelsea was soaking her feet in.

Ramón glanced up from the counter where he was arranging cookies on a rack with military precision. He had insisted on spending his one night off from the restaurant baking Christmas cookies. "Two people going to a Christmas ball together? That's pretty much a no-brainer."

"It's not a date," Chelsea insisted. "It's the skirt. Do I look like the kind of girl that wealthy bachelors invite to Christmas balls?"

"Why not?" Daryl asked.

"Because he's...because I'm..." pausing, Chelsea waved a hand in the air "...because we just don't mesh."

"Because you're attracted to him and you run from any man like that thanks to Boyd Carter," Daryl said, taking the pink polka-dotted piggy bank off the bookshelf and carrying it to her. "That's why you're pretending it's not a date."

Was she pretending? She *was* attracted to Zach McDaniels. But he was everything her mother had ever warned her about in a man—rich, handsome, the kind of man who would eventually walk away because she just didn't fit into his world. That was the only description her mother had ever given her of her father.

Daryl waved the piggy bank in front of her eyes. "Remember the rule. If it walks like a duck... Help me out here, Ramón."

"And if it talks like a duck..." Ramón said.

Chelsea found herself looking into two very determined pairs of eyes. Ramón had even paused in the act of shooting tiny bullets of green frosting at his row of cookies. They'd made a pact not to date and the fine for accepting one was twenty dollars. The funds they collected were to be spent on fixing up the place. That was Daryl's passion. And buying food for the times when they entertained. That was Ramón's passion. The pink piggy had a very hungry expression on her face. "All right." Chelsea gave in. "It is a duck."

"A date you mean," Daryl said, shaking the piggy at her again.

"Fine. A date," she agreed as she fished in her purse and finally stuffed a twenty-dollar bill into the waiting mouth. "But I'm telling you that the only reason I'm going is because I intend to get an article out of it. I'm wearing the skirt."

"You're what?" Daryl said, shock clear on his face.

"I'm going to wear the skirt to the ball."

Daryl frowned at the piece of black clothing which he'd draped over a chair near the fireplace. "You can't be serious."

"I'm depending on you to think of something."

"Do I look like Cinderella's fairy godmother?" Grinning, Daryl waved a hand. "On second thought, don't answer that."

"Please. It will make a great article."

"It will take a great miracle."

Chelsea bit back a sigh of relief as Daryl moved to the skirt and began to examine it, rubbing the material between his fingers.

"There's a beaded top I saw at the last Versace show. I could copy that and with the right pair of shoes..."

Behind her, Ramón laid down his frosting gun. "Who wants a pizza?"

Daryl shook his head. "Junk food. A master chef and that's all you eat, Ramón."

"Pizza meets all the requirements of the food pyramid," Chelsea said, suddenly realizing that she was starved. "Count me in."

"No anchovies," Daryl warned.

"The message light is on," Ramón said. "You both know the rule. The first one home is supposed to check the messages."

Chelsea met Daryl's eyes and rolled hers.

The first voice to pour out of the machine was Ramón's in command mode. "Leave a message."

The next voice was deeper pitched and raspy, barely more than a whisper.

"Your articles in *Metropolitan* are disgusting. Smut like that should be stopped. And so should the writer."

Despite the fact that her feet were soaking in hot water and the fire was burning brightly in the fireplace, Chelsea felt her skin turn ice-cold. "Who?" she asked, looking at Ramón.

"The caller ID says 'Out of Area.'"

Daryl sat down next to her on the couch. "Not to worry. There are a lot of freaks in the world. Some of them get their kicks scaring people. The anonymous ones are always cowards."

Chelsea put her hand over his. "I'm not afraid. I'm angry. And starved. Order that pizza, Ramón."

He was reaching for the receiver when the phone rang. Frowning, he lifted it to his ear and listened. "Who is this?"

Chelsea watched the expression on his face lighten. "Really? I'll put her on." Ramón passed her the phone. "He claims to be somebody from WNY's *Good Morning, New York* show. Let us know if he isn't and we'll handle it."

Lifting the receiver to her ear, she said. "Chelsea Brockway here... Yes, I'm the one who wrote the 'Hottie' articles for *Metropolitan*." Her eyes widened as she listened to what the man had to say. "Sure. I'll be waiting."

The moment she hung up the phone, she turned to her roommates. "That was James McCarthy, the host of

the show. He wants to interview me on Friday and he's
sending a limo for me at 5:00 a.m."

"You go girl!" Daryl said.

"Ditto," echoed Ramón.

"I'm going to wear the skirt." Chelsea said. "Do you
suppose it might work over the airwaves?"

6

"ZACH? ARE YOU AWAKE?"

"Yes." At 7:00 a.m., Zach was not only awake, but he'd already finished his morning workout and meditation. What surprised him was that his aunt Miranda was up. "What's wrong?"

"Turn on your TV. Hurry."

Striding into the living room of his apartment, Zach snagged the remote and pressed a button. "What is so important that you're watching TV at this hour?"

He heard a muffled groan from the other end. "I'm on my treadmill. TV makes it slightly less boring and you'll never guess. It's that woman you rescued in the bar the other day. She's on the WNY *Good Morning, New York* show."

"Which channel?" Zach asked.

"Five. She's talking about the articles she's going to be writing for *Metropolitan*."

Frowning, Zach pressed another button and a picture sprang to life—Chelsea Brockway sitting in front of a fireplace, chatting cozily with a handsome young man who had the slick good looks and toothy smile of a typical TV news anchor.

He'd missed her. That simple realization deepened

his frown. While his aunt chattered on in his ear, he had ample opportunity to notice that she was wearing the skirt and that it was hiked up a good two inches above her knee.

He'd purposely kept away from her for four days. Oh, she'd delivered her article right on time. Esme had put it on his desk just as soon as she'd sent it off to the printers. He'd found Chelsea had a knack for creating vivid vignettes laced with humor and a very deft hand at creating character. The wickedly accurate picture she'd drawn of the Texans had made him laugh out loud. He'd been much less comfortable with her portrait of the man who'd impulsively rushed to her rescue.

From start to finish her personality, her fresh style of seeing things had shone through.

It suddenly struck him that he'd been missing her all this time. That was why he hadn't been able to get her out of his mind.

Watching her laugh at something Mr. Teeth had just said to her, he felt the sharp twist in his gut and he had to acknowledge once again what he'd known from the first moment he'd seen her. He wanted her. Not seeing her for four days hadn't changed that one bit. Weighing the pluses and minuses of pursuing a relationship with her hadn't worked either. He hadn't even been able to come up with a decent list. How could he be with a woman as unpredictable as Chelsea? A woman who'd get herself on a morning talk show to promote her skirt articles without even clearing it with him!

"She's the woman Esme bought those articles from. The one I mentioned at lunch on Monday. Why didn't you tell me that?"

"I didn't know at the time," Zach said.

"She just mentioned that she has another article in the issue that hits the streets today and a contract for two more. I thought you were taking the magazine in a new direction?"

"I was. I am." When Mr. Teeth reached over to put a hand on Chelsea, Zach strode closer to the TV and pumped the volume button on his remote.

"She's talking about a skirt that attracts men," Miranda said.

The camera moved in for a close-up on Chelsea as she explained the history of the skirt to the viewing audience. Zach couldn't help but think that some island con artist had really done a snow job on her college roommate. Then she went on to compare it to "lucky" hats and shirts. She even had Mr. Teeth admitting that he wore a special tie when he had challenging interviews to do.

"She's good," Miranda said in his ear.

Too good. Zach had to hand it to Chelsea. She was making a man-magnet skirt sound like a real possibility.

And she was laughing and talking with Mr. Teeth as if they were on a date.

"That was a smart move on your part to get her on TV to promote the articles," Miranda said.

"I didn't," Zach said, not adding that the last thing he wanted to do was promote the skirt articles.

"Whoever did is a genius. Ninety percent of the single women in Manhattan are going to want to borrow that skirt. And they're bound to want to read *Metropolitan* to find out more about it. Do you know how many people in this city watch *Good Morning, New York?*"

Zach preferred not to think about it. His aunt's chatter in his ear nearly caused him to miss the shift that Chelsea's interview had taken.

"...mind if I ask you a few questions about your last article in *Metropolitan*, 'Hanging out for a Hottie?' Could you define what a *hottie* is, Chelsea?"

"*Hottie* is just the current term for every woman's dream guy," Chelsea said.

"But you've got to admit that *hottie* carries a certain sexual connotation that dream man doesn't."

"Absolutely."

"While I can't really ask you to be more specific on morning television, my staff has made up a list of people, most of them fairly well-known. We thought since you're the expert, you could let us know how they rate on the *hottie* scale. That way our viewing audience will have a better idea of what the term means without hurting our G-rating."

Once again the camera focused on Chelsea as the show's host began reading names. The first few were movie stars and politicians.

"I want to meet her," Miranda said. "Can you arrange it?"

"Tomorrow night. I'm taking her to your ball."

There was a small beat before Miranda said, "I can't wait to talk to her."

He was going to have a little talk with her himself.

Suddenly, his attention was riveted on the TV screen. It was his own picture he was staring at.

"Come on, Chelsea. You're starting to hedge on some of these people. You're the expert."

"I haven't met all of them in person. Sometimes you have to in order to be able to tell if they're really a *hottie*."

"Okay. Our viewing audience is looking at a picture of Zachary McDaniels, your new boss at *Metropolitan*. Have you met him in person?"

"Yes," Chelsea said.

"Is he a *hottie*?"

"Yes," Chelsea said without so much as a blink. "Definitely."

With Miranda's delighted laugh ringing in his ear, Zach watched his picture be replaced by a shot of the show's host grinning at the camera. "You heard it here, New York. Our expert here tells us that the new editor-in-chief of *Metropolitan* magazine is a *hottie*. Mr. Mc-Daniels, if you're watching, I want to invite you to come on this show next Tuesday, the day after Christmas, to respond to Chelsea's opinion." He winked at the camera. "And you'll have your chance to get in on the fun, New York. All day today and over the Christmas weekend, you can vote on whether or not you think Zach McDaniels is a *hottie* by simply accessing our Web site. We'll have the results for you next time we meet." He tapped two fingers to his head in a little salute. "Time's up for today. Good morning, New York."

Miranda was still laughing as the picture faded from the screen and an advertisement flashed on.

"Do you know how many people will be tuning in on Tuesday to find out the results *and* to see if you accept the challenge?"

Zach definitely did not want to think about that.

"THANKS A LOT, Ms. Brockway," said the young production assistant as she led the way toward a bank of elevators. "Mr. McCarthy is very happy with the segment, and it was sweet of you to sign autographs for those Cub Scouts. They certainly were fascinated by your skirt."

The moment the elevator doors closed, Daryl wrapped Chelsea in a big hug. "You were marvelous!"

Chelsea shook her head. "Somehow, I do not think that Zachary McDaniels is going to be enthused about being identified as a *hottie*."

"What else could you do?" Daryl said. "He's your boss. Are you supposed to tell the whole world that he's not a *hottie*? Believe me, given those two choices, you did the right thing, Chels."

"He's not going to think so. I can see the expression on his face right now." That was part of the problem, Chelsea thought as the elevator doors slid open and they stepped out onto the marble floor of the lobby.

She could picture too clearly every single one of Zach's expressions in her mind—the way his mouth curved when he laughed, the heat in those dark eyes when he'd been about to kiss her.

"Are you kidding? He's going to be laughing all the way to the bank. *Metropolitan* hits the streets today and any woman who saw you this morning is going to grab it off the stands. A magic skirt that attracts men? I'm seriously thinking of designing some knockoffs of this little number myself. Besides, the man asked you out on a date."

"No," Chelsea said, shaking her head. "He asked the skirt out."

Daryl stopped short in front of the revolving door and turned to face her. "You can't be serious."

"I am."

Daryl put his hands on her shoulders and lowered his face so that they were eye to eye. "The only magic about that skirt is the way I make it look on you."

"You're great, Daryl, but I've given it a lot of thought. He hasn't called me or tried to see me for four days. So when I was with him before, he was under the influence of the skirt. Now he's recovered."

With an impatient sigh, Daryl drew her away from the door and turned her so that she could see her reflection in the wall of glass that looked out on Madison Avenue.

"Get real, Chels. The man asked you out because of you. You're sweet, you're intelligent and even when I'm not dressing you, you're not bad on the eyes.

You're letting a bad experience with a total jerk ruin your self-image."

"He hasn't called."

"Knock, knock, Chels. This is the new millennium. You can call him. Or better still, go see him at his office. You can use the excuse of taking back his jacket—and then graciously accept his thanks for getting his magazine the kind of publicity that can't be bought." Taking her arm, Daryl led her toward the revolving doors.

"You think he'll see it that way?"

"I know he will," he said as they pushed their way to the sidewalk. "While you're there, you might mention the phone messages you've been getting."

Chelsea frowned at him even as a sliver of fear shot up her spine. There'd been one threatening call each day since the original that they'd listened to on Monday night. The voice was always muffled, the words the same. "Your articles in *Metropolitan* are disgusting. Smut like that should be stopped. And so should the writer."

She didn't like to think about the calls, didn't want to admit to either of her roommates that they were beginning to worry her. "We decided that it's just a crank."

Daryl shrugged. "Maybe. But it never hurts to have the boss worried about you."

As HE STRODE toward his office, Zach was cursing the stars he was born under.

"Morning, Mr. McDaniels." Linda Parker rose from her desk to hand him a stack of letters and messages.

"Your brother has called twice. I don't think he believed me when I told him you weren't in yet."

"If he calls again, tell him I'm in a meeting, and you can't interrupt me. And get Ms. Chelsea Brockway on the phone for me."

"Wasn't she wonderful this morning?"

Zach turned back from his door to study his secretary, a neat young woman in her mid-twenties with a sleek cap of brown hair. "You watched the show?"

She nodded. "I watch it every day. It was a great idea of yours to get Ms. Brockway on it. We've all been talking about it."

Zach glanced around quickly to see that three women at a nearby water cooler were looking in his direction. No, not looking. They were staring. One of them raised her cup in a salute. The other two were grinning ear to ear.

Linda Parker cleared her throat. "Several women have called, sir. I bet there'll be even more calls on the day that you appear. There isn't a woman in New York who won't want to see just what you look like in person."

"I—" But before Zach could correct her mistaken notion that he was going to appear on WNY, her phone rang.

"Zachary McDaniels's office." Pausing, she shot Zach a smile. "No, I can't put you through because he's in a meeting. Yes, I'll be sure he gets all of your messages, Mr. McDaniels."

Stepping into his office, he strode toward his desk

and began to sort through the messages. Two calls from his brother, who never called. Another from James McCarthy at WNY, the rest were from women whose names he didn't recognize. Women who were interested in meeting a *hottie?*

Chelsea Brockway had a lot to answer for.

Tossing the pink slips on his desk, he glanced at the plain white envelope that had been at the bottom of the phone messages. It bore no stamp or address, merely his name, printed in block letters and beneath that the word Private. Curious, he tore it open. Words had been cut and pasted together from the glossy pages of magazines.

Stop printing trash. Those who peddle sex shall perish. Monday night was just a warning.

Great. On top of everything, there was now a crank out there who was threatening him. How in the hell had the note gotten to his secretary? He strode quickly to his door and opened it.

"I'm dialing Ms. Brockway's number right now."

"Where did this envelope come from?"

Bending down, Linda Parker lifted a delivery envelope out of her wastebasket. "Excel Delivery."

"See if you can find out who sent it."

"Shall I leave a message on Ms. Brockway's machine?"

Zach nodded and closed his door. He'd barely had time to cross to his desk when his intercom sounded. "Yes?"

"She's here, sir—in reception. Ms. Brockway, I mean. Should I tell her you're in a—"

"Send her right in, Ms. Parker."

He'd taken two steps toward the door when he stopped himself and walked back to his desk. What was the matter with him? He was angry with her, not anxious to see her. What about the plan he'd come up with while he was getting dressed? He was going to do what he should have done in the first place—get her to tear up her contract for a generous settlement, of course. The moment he heard the door open and close behind him, he set the envelope down on his desk and turned to face her. He thought he had prepared himself. But one look was enough to tell him that staying away from her for four days had done nothing to lessen the desire that was spiraling through him. In the neat little blazer and blouse, she looked as young and innocent as a schoolgirl in uniform. He still wanted her. Hell, he wanted to grab her and ravish her on his father's desk. Better still, he wanted to take her on a secluded beach in the moonlight with palm trees whispering overhead and the ocean pounding. No one would interrupt them when he took her…again…and again. The vividness of the image had him moving forward, but the raw ache of the need crawling through him made him stop short.

This was the woman who was single-handedly deep-sixing his plans for *Metropolitan*.

"I wanted to return your jacket," she said. "If it's not a good time—"

"What the hell were you thinking, going on that show?" He took two steps before he stopped himself again. He was going to keep his distance, be rational and stick to his plan...even if it killed him.

"You're angry."

"You're perceptive."

She moved toward him, her chin lifting. "You know, you couldn't buy the kind of publicity I got for your magazine this morning."

"Publicity? Notoriety is a better word. How am I supposed to take this magazine in the direction I want to when you've undermined all the credibility I was hoping to establish by labeling me a...a *hottie*? I've had a phone call from that character with all the teeth who hosts the show. He probably expects me to come on his program and what? Offer a rebuttal?"

"Should I have said you're not a *hottie*?"

"What I would have preferred is that you hadn't gone on that show to further your own career goals at the expense of my magazine."

He was close enough to see her flinch, more than close enough to see the hurt flash into her eyes. He knew it was a mistake, but he reached for her anyway. "This is impossible!" He wanted to shake her. But he wanted to kiss her more. So he pulled her against him and closed his mouth over hers.

NO MAN SHOULD be able to move that fast. No man should be able to kiss like that—his mouth so hot, so hard, so irresistible. But he could. He did.

Even as the twin realizations swirled through her mind, she dropped the jacket she was holding, grabbed his shoulders and held on.

The anger she tasted on his tongue, felt in his hands where he gripped her, only seemed to add to the excitement streaming through her. She hadn't come here for this, she told herself as she threaded her fingers through his hair. But the moment he touched her, the moment she felt his mouth move on hers, she wanted him. It was simple. Primitive. And absolutely terrifying!

Her mother had warned her that someday she'd meet a man like this—one who would make her throw caution and planning, hopes and dreams to the wind. Someone who was absolutely impossible for her.

But even as she tried to gather the will to pull back, her hands tightened in the back of his neck to pull him closer.

"How dare you disgrace our father?"

The loud, booming voice penetrated her mind at the same moment that she felt Zach's hands grip her shoulders and set her from him.

7

"CHELSEA, I'd like you to meet my brother, Jeremiah McDaniels, the future governor of New York State. Jerry, this is—"

"I know who she is." Jerry McDaniels shot Chelsea a dismissive frown before he focused his attention back on Zach. "I cannot allow this."

"You can't allow me to kiss a woman? I didn't know your political agenda stretched so far as to outlaw kissing."

Chelsea glanced sideways at Zach. He was smiling, but not relaxed, and Jerry McDaniels's face was growing redder as he drew in a breath and let it out. It had taken her a moment to recognize him as the Long Island congressman who'd recently thrown his hat in the gubernatorial race. Not once had it occurred to her that he was related to Zach. They were so different. The older man was pompous, polished, preachy. Every gesture he made in the spots she'd seen on TV seemed choreographed. In comparison, Zach seemed almost spontaneous. Yet there were similarities, she realized as she glanced from one to the other. They both preferred to be in control and they both had tempers that were building to flash point.

"That's not what I'm talking about," Jerry said. "You can indulge in any kind of hanky-panky you want. While it doesn't surprise me, I certainly don't approve of your doing it in Father's office."

"It's my office now."

Jerry glared at him. "It won't be much longer if I have anything to do with it. I held my peace when Miranda told me she planned to turn the magazine over to you. I was hoping you'd changed. Either that or you'd tire of running it and move on to some other hobby before you did any real damage. But I can't stand by and allow you to smear our father's name by turning his magazine into some kind of trash-filled tabloid that peddles sex."

"Now wait just a moment—" Zach began.

Instinctively, Chelsea stepped between the two men. The one thing she did know about was brothers when they were in a temper. "Stop it right now! Your father wouldn't want you to fight. Not in his office."

"My office," Zach said.

When he gripped her arms and tried to set her aside, Chelsea sagged against him.

Jerry took a step back. "I don't fight. I don't fight because I'm a peaceful man. I just came here to inform you that I can no longer in good conscience give you my support. I've arranged for the board of McDaniels Inc. to meet in emergency session on Tuesday afternoon and I'm going to call for your resignation."

"I won't resign," Zach said.

"Then I'll ask to have you removed. As a candidate

running on family values, I can't condone what you're doing to *Metropolitan*."

"Family values?" Chelsea asked, straightening. "How can you pass yourself off as someone who supports family values when you're stabbing your own brother in the back?"

Jerry frowned at her. "I do not intend to be lectured to by a woman who is writing articles about *hotties* and a sex-magnet skirt...." His sentence trailed off as he glanced down at the article of clothing in question. "Or who parades around in something that..."

Chelsea found herself staring as his face reddened and he struggled to swallow.

"...something that advertises easily, available...oh my...I...." Drawing in a deep breath, he wrenched his gaze from the skirt and met her eyes. "That's it—the skirt..."

"Forget the skirt. Just let Zach explain."

Jerry backed two quick steps away from her. Chelsea followed him.

"He'll tell you that he didn't have anything to do with my articles. Or my appearance on *Good Morning, New York*. He even tried to buy out my contract."

"But he didn't and considering what I saw a few minutes ago and what I'm seeing now..." Backing into the door, Jerry grabbed the knob and yanked it open. "It's pretty clear why."

"Wait..." Only the fact that Zach grabbed her by the arm prevented her from following Jerry out of the office.

"It's no use," he said, shoving the door shut behind his brother.

"Well! No wonder you told me you were an only child. If he were my brother, I'd be in deep denial over him, too!"

Zach stared at her for a moment, then suddenly threw back his head and laughed. The rich, bright sound filling the office was so infectious that Chelsea couldn't help but join him.

"It's not really funny," she said, pressing her hand to her stomach. Yet she couldn't help but admire Zach for looking at the humorous side of the situation.

"Did you see the way he looked at your skirt?"

"As if it were going to bite him?" This time she put more effort into pushing down a fresh wave of laughter. "You have to go after him, make him listen. He'll change his mind once he understands what you want to do with *Metropolitan*."

Zach shook his head, his smile fading. "It won't make any difference. Jerry has his own agenda and he doesn't want me here. This business with the skirt on TV has just given him the opportunity he wants to get rid of me."

Chelsea put a hand on his arm. "You can't let him. Surely there's something you can do." The instant the thought hit her, she smiled. "I know. You could accept that invitation to go on *Good Morning, New York*. It would give you an opportunity to explain to everyone what you intend to do with the magazine."

ZACH STUDIED HER for a minute. There was a part of him that wanted to believe that Chelsea Brockway also had her own agenda. If he went on the morning TV show, her articles would garner even more attention and she'd get more of the name recognition that she wanted.

But there was another part of him that doubted she could come up with anything as structured or organized as an agenda. There was a fundamental honesty about her. It was part of what made her writing so appealing. And the concern in her eyes was real. He was sure of it. Just as real as the feelings her concern triggered in him.

He couldn't recall the last time someone had defended him with any member of his family. Not even Miranda had had the courage to go up against his father when he was alive.

And it wasn't the first time she'd wedged herself between him and someone who wanted to take a punch at him, he recalled with a sudden frown. "You're going to have to stop doing that."

"What?"

"Getting in between me and someone who wants to hit me."

"It's an old habit. I had to baby-sit my three brothers every day after school. It was my job to see that they didn't kill each other. Getting in between them was usually my most effective option."

Tilting his head, he studied her for a moment. "Usually?"

Grinning at the memory, she rubbed her hand against her side. "My timing was a little off once and I got a cracked rib. The doctor said I was lucky I didn't get a shiner or a broken nose."

Without thinking, Zach lifted his hand and ran his finger down her nose. "That would have been a shame."

It was a mistake to touch her. The brief contact had him instantly hungry for more. He couldn't seem to prevent his fingers from tracing the curve of her cheek, then moving lower to feel her pulse quicken in that soft hollow at the base of her throat. Her eyes were wide and locked on his. Even as he watched, they darkened. Her lips were parted, moist. He had only to lean down, close that small distance between them and he could taste her again. He watched her draw in a breath, listened to it shudder out. It was the sound of surrender and he felt an ache, gnawing and sweet move through him.

How he wanted to really touch her, to slip her out of that neat little blazer and unfasten the buttons on that schoolgirl blouse one at a time. Then his hands could slip over every inch of that soft skin, molding it slowly, very slowly. As the images filled his mind, the ache moving through him twisted sharply into need. No woman had ever pulled at him this way before. What was it about her? He should be thinking about ways to stop his brother from turning the board of McDaniels Inc. against him, not thinking about what it would be like to make love with Chelsea Brockway in his father's office.

No, it was *his* office, Zach reminded himself. And it could slip away from him if he wasn't careful. The woman standing in front of him posed a threat to his dream. He should be thinking of ways to get her out of his life.

"This has to stop," he said.

"Hmmm?"

The fact that her eyes were still cloudy, still fixed on his nearly undermined his intent. "I want you, Chelsea Brockway." There, he'd said it out loud. Now, perhaps he could summon up some common sense and deal with the problem. There were so many minuses to pursuing a relationship with her. Hadn't he listed them all? He tried to bring them to mind, but if he looked one more minute into those eyes, he was going to...

Thrusting his hands into his pockets, Zach took a step back from her.

Chelsea blinked and took a quick step back from him, too. "It's the skirt."

Zach's eyes narrowed. "What are you talking about?"

"You just said you wanted me. I want you, too. A few seconds ago when you touched me I...I...it's got to be the skirt."

"You can't be serious."

"What other explanation could there be?"

"Chemistry. Lust. You're a desirable woman. I'm a man." There. He'd been right. Putting something into words made it much less...scary? No, wrong word. He certainly wasn't afraid. Not of a woman or a skirt.

"I didn't want to believe it at first either, but you've got to admit, it's had a pretty strange effect on almost every man I've run into...even your brother. I thought for a minute he was going to have an attack."

Zach raised his brows. "My brother's a little stuffy, but he's not dead. When you wear a skirt that everyone can see right through, it's bound to have an effect on the male of the species."

Leaning down, Chelsea lifted the hem of the skirt. "What are you talking about? This material is perfectly opaque. Look. You can't even see my fingers through it."

He couldn't. He was about to tell her that she had to stand with the light behind her, but the moment she'd touched the skirt, he'd caught her scent again.

You'll never let her go...

Zach pushed the words firmly out of his mind. "This whole conversation is ridiculous. What I'm feeling, what we're feeling has nothing to do with a skirt that some island woman conned your roommate into buying. It has everything to do with the fact that we simply want each other and we have to decide what to do about it."

For a moment neither of them spoke. He wasn't even touching her. In fact, he was standing a good two feet away from her. But he knew exactly what he wanted to do. The urge to move forward was so strong that he clenched his hands into fists at his side to keep from reaching for her.

He wasn't even sure how long he'd stood there struggling before the sharp buzz of the intercom on his desk seemed to set him free.

CHELSEA ONLY let out the breath she was holding when Zach had put the desk between them and pressed the button on his phone. "What is it?"

"It's your aunt." Ms. Parker's clear, crisp voice filled the room. "She's right here at my desk, and she insisted that I buzz you even though I told her you were in a meeting and couldn't be disturbed."

"I can always be disturbed for my aunt Miranda," Zach said, a smile tugging at the corners of his mouth.

Chelsea stepped out of the way of the door as it swung open and a tall woman in a bright green suit breezed into the room. She barely had time to register that it was the same woman who'd been with Zach in the restaurant that first day before Zach moved forward to embrace his aunt warmly.

With their heads so close together, Chelsea couldn't help but notice the strong resemblance. They had the same dark hair, the same striking features. Though the woman was clearly older, the two looked more like brother and sister than aunt and nephew. When Miranda drew back, smiling up at Zach and patting him on the cheek, Chelsea decided to like her on the spot.

"That was exactly the right thing to say to Ms. Parker," Miranda said "Now I have one more thing to add to my list of why you're my favorite nephew and Jerry isn't."

"You ran into my charming brother, I take it," Zach murmured.

Miranda's smile faded as she fisted her hands on her hips. "He was here?"

"He just left."

Her foot began to tap. "He's a very lucky man. If I could get my hands on him I might strangle him. The moment I got home from the gym, I started getting calls from board members demanding that I call an emergency meeting. Jerry has them all stirred up over Ms. Brockway's appearance on *Good Morning, New York.* I told them the earliest meeting I could call would be Tuesday afternoon. They'll have time to cool off by then. And hopefully, I will have overcome my urge to do him some kind of physical harm."

Zach grinned. "I can sympathize with your sentiments when it comes to Jerry, but it's me he wants to run out of town, not you."

Miranda tapped a finger on her chest. "*I'm* the one he sandbagged. When I told him that I was going to turn *Metropolitan* over to you to run, he swore to me that you would have his support, that he wouldn't lobby board members behind my back."

"According to Jerry, he did support me, but now I've blown it."

Miranda made a very unladylike snort. "In less than a week? No, he just pretended to go along with me. He bided his time, waiting for some issue to pop up so that he could blow it all out of proportion and use it to try to boot you off the magazine and promote himself as a family-values candidate at the same time. I know when I've been sandbagged—and I just hate it!"

"Does he have that much power with the board?" Zach asked.

Miranda frowned. "Yes. He's an excellent politician. He knows just how to play the members of the board. But in this instance, he has underestimated his opposition. I'm a pretty good politician myself. And I have a plan!"

"I never doubted it for a moment."

"First, you're going on *Good Morning, New York* on Tuesday."

Zach raised his hands. "Whoa! Stop right there. I have no intention of going on that show."

Miranda tapped her finger on his chest. "You have to. It's the perfect opportunity for you to set the record straight and let everyone know the direction you intend to take *Metropolitan*. The timing will be perfect, just before the board meeting. Besides, whose message do you want the world to hear—yours or Jerry's?"

"I don't like it."

"Think of it this way. Your brother is going to like it even less. In the meantime, I'm going to manipulate the seating at my Christmas ball tomorrow night so that certain board members are at my table. That will give them a chance to get reacquainted with you. And I want that Ms. Brockway's phone number, so that I can persuade her to wear the skirt."

"Why don't you ask her right now?" Zach took his aunt's arm and turned her so that she could see Chelsea. "Aunt Miranda, I'd like you to meet Chelsea Brockway."

Miranda moved forward with her hand extended. "Whoops! I didn't even see you there. I've been so wanting to meet you. Please, tell me I haven't said anything terribly indiscreet."

Chelsea found herself returning the smile of the older woman as she grasped her hand. "How about if I promise not to repeat anything I heard?"

Miranda glanced at Zach. "I love her." Then she turned her attention back to Chelsea. "Zach tells me that you're coming to my Christmas ball. I hope you'll wear the skirt. I can't wait to see it."

"You're looking at it," Chelsea said.

Miranda glanced down. "That's it?"

Chelsea nodded.

"But it looks so...ordinary. I mean, it's quite lovely— simple, basic, versatile." As she spoke, Miranda began to move around Chelsea in a circle. Suddenly, she stopped. "Wait. Isn't that the same skirt that you were wearing the other day in the restaurant—the one the bartender was fussing with?"

Chelsea nodded. "That was my roommate Daryl. He's studying fashion design and he fastened it up with tape. He put staples in the waistband."

"Staples? How clever!"

"They hold pretty well—except when I run. I nearly

lost it the other night when Zach and I were trying to escape from those Texans in the bar."

"The Texans in your article? Zach was the man who helped you escape from them?" Miranda asked, glancing at her nephew.

"Exactly," Chelsea said. "If it wasn't for him, I'm sure the skirt would have done me in. I never would have been able to move fast enough to get out of the way of that car. It nearly ran us down."

"The *car*," Zach said, frowning as he moved to the desk. "I'd nearly forgotten about that."

Miranda's brows shot up. "That skirt must really have a special power if it makes you forget about being nearly run down."

Lifting the white envelope, Zach slipped the message out. "This was in my pile of messages this morning. 'Stop printing trash. Those who peddle sex shall perish. Monday night was just a warning.' I didn't put it together until just now, but the writer could be referring to that car."

Chelsea stared as Miranda moved to look at the paper in Zach's hands. As he'd read the threat aloud, her throat had frozen. She made herself draw in a deep breath and let it out. On the ride to Zach's office, she'd managed to convince herself that Daryl was being overprotective. All week, she had tried not to think about the messages. And she didn't want to talk about them. Putting things into words always made them more real. More frightening. But if Zach were being threatened, too... Drawing in another deep breath, she said, "I've been getting messages like that on my answering machine all week."

"What?" Zach and his aunt both turned to stare at her.

"One message a day starting Monday night."

"You were being threatened and you didn't think to tell me?" Zach asked.

The sharpness of his tone had her twisting her fingers together. "I thought it was just a crank."

For a moment Zach didn't reply, but the anger in his eyes was very real. And it was her fault. Because of her articles, he was receiving threatening notes and a car had nearly run him down. She took a deep breath. "Look, I'm sorry I didn't tell you about the phone calls sooner. I didn't think—" she raised a hand and then dropped it. "And I'm sorry that I'm causing you problems with your family and the board of directors. Maybe it would be better all around if I didn't write any more articles about the skirt."

For a moment there was complete silence in the room. Miranda was staring at her. Zach's eyes had narrowed.

"What exactly are you saying?" he asked.

Chelsea moistened her lips. "Why don't I just tear my contract up?"

"No." Zach's tone was flat and final.

It was her turn to stare. "But you...you don't want to print them. On Monday, you offered to buy me out."

Zach waved the letter that he held in his hand. "What kind of editor would I be if I let someone dictate what I'm going to print by threatening me? No. You're going to write the articles and I'm going to print them."

"But you could be in danger," Chelsea said.

"So could you. So we're going to take precautions. I'll hire you a bodyguard."

"It sounds like you both need one," Miranda said, opening her purse. "I have the card of the security firm I'm using at my ball. They're excellent and they could investigate who's behind the threats."

Zach slipped the card she handed him into his pocket, but his eyes never left Chelsea's. "I'll have Ms. Parker make the arrangements."

Chelsea rose from her chair. "It's not just about the threats. You could get fired from your job."

"Mr. McDaniels."

The moment Zach shifted his gaze beyond her, Chelsea turned to see his secretary standing just inside the office door.

"What is it?" Zach snapped.

"I'm sorry. I know you said not to interrupt you, and I didn't want to buzz you again. But Ms. Sinclair just called. You were due in the staff meeting twenty minutes ago. She says it's very important that you come right away. There's a problem."

Zach glanced at his aunt. "I'll bet that board members aren't the only people Jerry's lobbying."

"Do you want me to come with you?" Miranda asked.

"I can handle them."

"Tell them that I've torn up my contract," Chelsea said.

"We've settled that. I don't want you to leave until Ms. Parker makes the arrangements with the security firm."

Chelsea had her mouth open, ready to argue when Miranda said, "I've got a better idea. Why don't I take Chelsea to lunch while you go to your staff meeting? By that time, the bodyguard should be here."

"Thanks." Zach gave his aunt a hug, then turned to Chelsea. "We're not finished."

Oh, yes they were, Chelsea promised herself. As soon as she could shake Miranda McDaniels loose, she was going to make sure that the skirt never bothered Zach again.

8

ESCAPE. Chelsea hadn't realized how badly she'd needed it until she finally watched Miranda McDaniels's taxi pull away from the curb. It had taken some doing, but she'd finally persuaded Zach's aunt that she was exhausted after getting up at 4:00 a.m. for a TV show and that she would be perfectly safe at home.

Of course, she'd had to fudge the exact details of her building's security system—which was handled by buzzers and not an actual person on duty. But no tenants had been burglarized since she and her roommates had moved in six months ago.

As Miranda's taxi disappeared around the corner, Chelsea turned back to her apartment building. It wasn't that she hadn't enjoyed her lunch at the Tavern on the Green. How often had she fantasized about eating there once she'd established herself? The well-known restaurant with its fairy-tale setting in Central Park contrasted sharply with the stark, tired-looking façade of her apartment building. Just looking at the faded bricks and crumbling front steps made her feel a little like Cinderella coming home from the ball.

A perfect analogy, she thought as a sharp wind slapped a flurry of icy snowflakes against her cheeks. She'd better keep in mind that there'd be a midnight to deal with when it came to the skirt.

She sent it a frown as she fished in her pocket for her key. Miranda had been convinced that the skirt had been working its magic at the restaurant. Several men had dropped by their table. Though she'd been introduced to each one, she'd lost track of the names—except for one. Miranda had made a point of telling her that Harrison Marsh sat on the board at McDaniels Inc. Miranda had even invited him to join them for dessert. Mr. Marsh, a tall man with silver-gray hair and a matching goatee, had a face as impassive as the presidential carvings on Mount Rushmore.

As he'd sipped ponderously on a tiny cup of espresso, Chelsea had done her best to explain her appearance on the *Good Morning, New York* show and the skirt. She'd assured him that it had never been Zach's plan to publish her articles in the first place, that Esme Sinclair had offered her the contract and that Zach had done his best to buy her out.

Pushing her key into the lock, Chelsea replayed the scene in her mind as she'd been doing ever since the man had risen from the table and told her that he was looking forward to sharing a table with her at Miranda's Christmas ball. There was so much more that she could have said. Should have said. Each time she

went over it, she became more and more convinced
that she'd blown it.

Never mind that Miranda had been close to ecstatic,
claiming she'd never seen the "stone-faced" Mr. Marsh
so charmed by anyone before. Shivering, Chelsea used
her key on the second door and pushed her way into
the warmth of the lobby.

Miranda had said that she wasn't so sure it was
merely the skirt's doing, but she'd like to have one herself and give it a whirl.

It all came back to the skirt.

It was causing Zach business troubles. And it was
causing her heart trouble. It all boiled down to the fact
that she wanted Zach to want her even without the influence of the skirt.

And she was pretty sure he didn't. Wouldn't.

With a sigh, she turned her key in the mailbox and
removed its contents. Was this the way Cinderella felt
when she finally got home from the ball that night and
had to huddle on the hearth in her old rags? Did she
torture herself wondering if the prince would still love
her as she really was—without fairy godmothers and
magic?

Her plan when she'd left Zach's office this morning
was to go home, tear up her contract, put the skirt in a
box and mail it off to Kate or Gwen. Then she wouldn't
be tempted to use it again for another article—or for
Zach. That way he and his brother could find some
common ground.

But after Harrison Marsh had actually smiled at her, Miranda had made her promise to wear the skirt to the Christmas ball. If there was any chance that it could help Zach...

Tossing three circulars and two winning magazine sponsored lottery numbers into a nearby basket, Chelsea headed toward the elevator. Two of the remaining envelopes were bills and the third was a letter addressed to her. Tearing it open, she stepped into the waiting car and pressed a button. She was shooting upward when the cut out letters on the page registered in her mind.

Stop peddling sex. This is your last warning.

An icy sliver of fear shot down her spine, chilling her even more than the blustery December wind that had pushed her into the building. But as she stared down at the note, something else began to replace the fear, something hot that bubbled up from her core.

She was not going to run from someone who was so cowardly he couldn't sign his own name. Her anger buoyed her up and carried her all the way to the door of her apartment.

She was flipping through the keys on her ring when she noticed that the door wasn't closed tight. Her first thought was that Ramón had left for work in a hurry. Then she noticed that part of the doorjamb had splintered. This time the fear was even icier than before, numbing her throat, her lungs. Even as she stood there frozen, she thought she heard a faint sound from the other side of the door. The creak of a floorboard.

Dread filled her, sudden and sure. Someone was waiting for her in the apartment. She knew it. Not Daryl and not Ramón. They would be at the restaurant. Even as the panic bubbled up, she heard another creak, faint but unmistakable and something else—the brush of fabric against a wall? In her mind she pictured someone creeping slowly forward, moving down the short, narrow hallway, then stepping into the tiny foyer.

Chelsea focused all her energy on taking one careful step backward.

Whoever it was must have been waiting for her, listening. A deaf man could hear the elevator groan its way up five floors. Then he must have heard her fiddling with her keys.

He must be wondering right now why she wasn't inserting it in the lock and pushing the door open.

To fill the silence, she rattled her key ring again as she took another careful step back. Baby steps, she told herself. Take another and another. She knew how to do this, she'd done it hundreds of times when she'd played hide-and-seek with her younger brothers.

They'd never once caught her.

Three more steps and she reached the door to the stairs. It would creak, a noisy, earth shattering sound. Whoever it was waiting on the other side of that door would know that she knew.

Chelsea risked a quick glance over her shoulder. The

elevator doors were shut, but the five button was still lit. She breathed out a little prayer. The old car was noisy and slow, but it would still get her to the lobby faster than running down five flights of stairs. It would get a pursuer there faster, too.

It was the last thought that freed her to make a sprint for the elevator and press the button. The moment the doors started to open, she slid through them sideways, then waited an eternity before they shut again and the car let out a groan. Another eon passed before she stepped out into the lobby. She took one quick look around before she tore across it and pushed through the double set of doors into the street.

AT ONE O'CLOCK, Zach finally made his way out of the staff meeting. It hadn't gone well. They'd all seen or heard about Chelsea's interview on *Good Morning, New York*. They all knew that they could vote on whether or not their boss was a *hottie* simply by accessing WNY's Web site.

How could he have expected the meeting to go well when his entire staff wondered what in the hell he was doing with their magazine?

And it was theirs. He really hadn't given enough consideration to that. Esme had been standing at the head of the conference table where she'd obviously been running the meeting since he'd been late. She'd only moved when he'd sat down in the head chair, forcing her to take the one to his right.

One quick look around the room had allowed him to freeze-frame in his mind the expressions on the faces of his staff. Carleton Bushnell's face had been split by a wide grin. He thought that being voted a *hottie* was a great advertising ploy. But he stood alone in his delight.

Esme's face had been, as always, impassive. Hal Davidson had pointed out that *Metropolitan* was in danger of being classified as a tabloid. Was that the direction he intended to take them in? But it was Bill Anderson who'd asked him bluntly if he intended to resign at the emergency board meeting on Tuesday.

His negative reply hadn't pleased anyone that he could see.

He'd spent the next hour dodging more bullets. His denial that he had arranged Chelsea's interview hadn't placated them at all. They saw it as evidence that he wasn't in control.

From their point of view, he was single-handedly ruining their livelihood. He'd told them one thing and seemed to be doing another. That was not a stellar quality in a leader.

The meeting had ended on a final unhappy note—news that three longtime advertisers had canceled their ads because they no longer wanted to be associated with *Metropolitan*.

The only plus that he could see was that no one had resigned—yet. They probably didn't want to go home jobless three days before Christmas.

"Mr. McDaniels."

As he passed the water cooler, Ms. Parker fell into step beside him.

"Sorry, sir. I was just touching base with some of the other secretaries. You know, everyone in the office has voted."

"Voted?"

"On WNY's Web site. We want to make sure you win. The last time I checked, there were only a few negative votes. You know...it's kind of exciting to be working for someone who is..."

Zach's frown had her sentence trailing off.

"Did you make the arrangements with that security firm?" he asked.

She nodded as she moved behind her desk and turned his appointment calendar toward him. "A Mr. Romano will be meeting you here at seven-thirty tonight. That was the soonest that he could fit you in. He would have preferred to wait until after Christmas, but I told him that it was an emergency. I thought meeting here in the office would be more convenient for you since you usually work late."

"Fine. Did he assign someone to Ms. Brockway?"

Ms. Parker shook her head. "I told him that's what you wanted, but he said he'd be setting all that up after you talked."

Zach's frown deepened. He didn't like it, not one bit. "Where is Ms. Brockway now? Has my aunt called in?"

"Oh, yes. She said you're not to worry. She took Ms. Brockway back to her apartment in a taxi. Her building has a fine security system."

"Get Ms. Brockway for me," Zach said.

The phone rang just as Ms. Parker reached for it.

"Zach McDaniels's office. Yes, Ms. Brockway. He's right here."

He took the phone.

"Zach."

The thread of fear in her voice had his stomach knotting. "Are you all right?" *She was calling him. She had to be fine.*

"My apartment. Someone..."

"Where are you?"

"In a coffee shop. I panicked and ran."

He drew in a deep breath. Her words hadn't come quickly enough to prevent the image from flooding his mind—he could imagine her just as easily walking right into her apartment and...

He breathed deeply again and forced his voice to remain calm. "Good. You're safe." It helped to say the words aloud. "Tell me what happened."

"Someone was in my apartment. I think. The door was ajar—just a little—and the jamb was splintered. I thought I heard a noise. That's when I ran."

"Smart girl," Zach said, stifling several curses that were running through his mind. "Have you called the police?"

"No. I didn't think. I called you."

Other feelings washed through him, dissolving some of the fear.

"I should have called them. I'll do it right now."

"No, I'll take care of it. Tell me exactly where you are." Taking the pencil and paper that Ms. Parker pushed toward him, he jotted down the address.

"Now, I'm going to give you my cell phone number and I want you to call me right back on that phone." As soon as he'd rattled off the numbers and hung up the receiver, he began to count the seconds. He was at fifteen—plenty of time to imagine what might have happened to her in that apartment if she'd gone in, plenty of time to worry that something, someone was stopping her from calling back. Then his cell phone finally rang.

"Zach?" Her voice was much stronger this time.

It was his own that sounded thready with fear when he said, "I'm on my way."

SHE'D THOUGHT she was prepared. Zach had insisted that they wait until the police arrived before they went back into the building, so she'd had lots of time to steel herself for what lay behind her apartment door.

Still, she hadn't pictured *this*. In the face of the destruction, she was only able to absorb certain details— the cookies that Ramón had slaved over had been dumped out of their containers. The Christmas tree had tipped over on its side, the ornaments Daryl had been collecting for years lay smashed and scattered throughout the room. The mantel over the fireplace had been cleared. It was the one space in the room that wasn't littered with debris.

"Who?"

She hadn't realized how cold she was or how stiff until Zach pulled her into his arms and she felt his warmth. It was only then that the icy ball of fear that had formed in her stomach like a tight hard fist began to melt. Leaning into him seemed so natural, so right.

Uncurling her fingers, she pressed her palm flat against his chest. The steady thud of his heart began to relax her. Slowly, she began to absorb other sensations. The press of his hand as it moved up her spine, the hardness of his body as he molded her more closely against it. And his scent—he smelled like...Zach. For just a moment, she promised herself. She would let herself need this, depend on this.

As the seconds ticked away, she was aware of footsteps as the two detectives searched the other rooms. She could hear the apartment manager's intermittent mumbling and the squeak of his tennis shoes as he tagged after them. But the sounds seemed to come from far away. Chelsea felt as if an invisible protective shield had risen up around her and Zach. She couldn't put a name to the feelings seeping through her. But she wanted to hold on to them. She wanted to hold on to Zach.

"Have you got any enemies?"

The words pierced the bubble, but for a moment she

still didn't move. It was Zach who stepped back, his hands gently turning her so that she finally faced the stocky detective who had spoken. Perez. He'd introduced himself as Detective Perez.

"Chelsea?" Zach's hand tightened on hers.

"No. No enemies. Certainly no one who would do this. At least I didn't think so."

"Think about it," he said as he fished a notebook and pencil out of his coat.

"No thing like this ever happen before." The voice came from the apartment manager, a short balding man who had entered through the archway to the kitchen. Wringing his hands, he shot her an accusing glance. "No burglaries in this building for five years. I tell them."

"Is that true?" Zach directed his question at the detective.

The man grunted. "Could very well be. This isn't a high-crime neighborhood. But whoever did this wasn't a pro." He directed his own accusing glance at the manager. "Even a rookie could have picked the locks on these doors. He made a mess of it."

"This is secure building," the manager said, wringing his hands again. "This never happen here."

"Yeah, well, this place isn't exactly Fort Knox. It doesn't take a high-tech security expert to buzz apartments until he finds a sucker to let him in."

Chelsea found herself wanting to hug the rumpled-looking detective. The manager was beginning to remind her of a Greek chorus stuck on one gloomy refrain.

Perez bent down to pick up a crumpled bill from the floor. It was only as he unfolded the twenty that Chelsea recognized the shards of pottery that lay beneath it as Daryl's piggy bank. "Whoever it was missed this," he said.

"That's all there was in the bank," she said.

The detective met her gaze. "You telling me the perp broke the bank but left the money?"

"He must have. There was only one twenty in it. It was mine."

"A burglar who wasn't interested in money. Curiouser and curiouser," said the detective.

"This never happen before."

"Right," Perez said, moving toward the manager. "Why don't you go back downstairs and call the owner. He'll want to be contacting his insurance company, don't you think?" After closing the door, he turned back to Chelsea. "It doesn't have the look of a robbery, either. It looks personal."

"It gets even more personal in the bedrooms," said his partner as she entered through the archway.

Chelsea guessed the woman detective to be in her mid-twenties and she was as neatly pressed and put together as her partner was rumpled.

"The clothes have been pulled out of all of the closets, but only the woman's have been slashed," she said.

"They slashed my clothes?" Chelsea asked, but

when she started toward the bedroom, Zack tightened his grip on her hand again.

"Do you have any idea why someone would do that?" the woman asked.

"No. I don't even know who," Chelsea said.

"Are you her boyfriend?" Perez directed his question at Zach.

"No," he said. "I'm her boss."

"You're not dating?" the detective asked.

"We have a date tomorrow night," Zack said.

"It's not really a date," Chelsea said quickly. "We're going to his aunt's Christmas ball."

"So you're not really dating him. But you're going to a ball with him tomorrow night?"

"That about sums it up," Zack said.

Chelsea could hear the laugh in his voice and she found she had to bite down on the inside of her cheek to keep from smiling. It wasn't funny. There was nothing to laugh at. But standing there, being grilled by a detective who reminded her of an old TV rerun, she felt a sudden kinship with Zach—as if they had both been hauled into the principal's office to face the music.

"Okay, who is your real boyfriend?" the detective asked. "What's his name?"

Chelsea glanced at Zach and found that he was looking at her. "I don't have one, not currently."

"Okay. How about an uncurrent one? The last one you went out with?" Perez said.

"Boyd Carter." *Zach knew Boyd.* She could tell by the way he stiffened beside her. Perez knew it too.

"How do you know this Carter guy?" he asked Zach.

"His father sits on my board of directors."

The detective closed his notebook. "Interesting. I don't know about you, Mr. McDaniels, but I want to take a look at the bedrooms."

Chelsea had taken two steps to follow them when the detective turned back to her. "I don't think it's a good idea for you to see this, Ms. Brockway. What would help us a great deal is if you could tell Detective Gray here about your relationship with Mr. Carter."

It was a very smart move, Chelsea thought as she watched Zach and the older man walk away. Now they could be grilled separately.

She wasn't looking forward to it one bit.

ZACH FOLLOWED Detective Perez down the short hallway and into the first room. It had been ransacked like the living room. The closet door was open and clothes had been yanked off the hangers and strewn every which way around the room. A chair had been overturned, a lamp smashed. The damage seemed sporadic, as if a child had succumbed to a temper tantrum.

But when they entered the next room, Zach stopped short in the doorway, and anger hit him like a two-fisted punch in the stomach.

The mattress had been ripped from the bed and

there was nothing left that could be identified as clothes. Just bits of lace, shreds of cloth. If Chelsea had been here... If she'd entered the apartment instead of running... The images streaming through his mind had the fear knotting tight in his stomach.

"Tell me about Boyd Carter," Perez said.

"You think he did this?"

"I don't think anything yet. My job is just to check out the possibilities."

Possibilities. Zach's mind was filled with them as his gaze swept the room. Then he saw the words scrawled on the mirror and fear became a sickness in his stomach.

Stop peddling sex. This is your last warning.

Peddling. Jerry had used that word. But he wouldn't... Clenching his hands into fists, Zach fought against the whirl of emotions raging through him and reached deep within himself for control. His brother hated him, but surely he couldn't have done this. If he had...

"I'm no psychologist, but whoever did this might be a victim of his own anger and jealousy," Perez said. "There are people who react in a very violent way when someone who used to be with them starts to date someone else."

Zach turned to the detective. "But why would Boyd Carter be jealous of me? Ms. Brockway and I haven't actually been out on a date."

"Yet." Perez gave him a level look. "Let's cut to the

chase, McDaniels. My wife's a faithful fan of *Good Morning, New York.* It's usually on when I grab a cup of coffee on the way out the door. I happened to catch Ms. Brockway when she identified you as a *hottie.* If this guy is the jealous type, that might be all it took to have him assume that your relationship is more than boss-employee. In these cases, we're not talking about someone whose satellite dish gets all the channels, if you know what I mean?"

"Yeah," Zach said, stuffing his hands in his pockets. "I just don't think—"

"You're not supposed to think. That's my job. Just tell me everything you know about this guy."

What he knew was damn little, Zach thought as he watched Perez close his notebook two minutes later. The detective was annoyed with him. Hell, he was annoyed with himself. He'd only met Boyd Carter at a few social functions that his aunt had dragged him to over the years. The only reason the name had rung a bell was because he'd made it his business to know who was sitting on the board of McDaniels Inc.

Could Carter be the crazed, jealous boyfriend that Perez suspected? If he was, could he be behind the notes and the attempted hit-and-run on Monday night? Or could it be Jerry...?

"You got any other candidates in mind for the crazy who did this?" Perez asked him.

For a second, Zach said nothing. Then he shook his

head. "No one comes to mind, but I'll let you know if I think of someone."

"You do that, McDaniels. In the meantime, I'm assuming you'll keep an eye on Ms. Brockway."

"You can bet on it," Zach said.

"I CAN'T STAY with you at your apartment," Chelsea said, bracing herself as the taxi came to a lurching stop at a traffic light.

"Before we get into that, tell me about Boyd Carter."

Chelsea sighed. "I'd rather not. Talking about him makes me feel stupid."

"Perez thinks he may have been the one who trashed your apartment."

Chelsea shook her head. "I told Detective Gray it wasn't Boyd. I simply wasn't that important to him." The taxi lurched forward, sending a pedestrian scurrying back to the curb.

"Where did you meet him?"

She sent him an exasperated glance. "You're just going to keep badgering me with questions aren't you?"

"Until you convince me that Carter didn't destroy your apartment. Where did you meet him?"

"In the restaurant where Daryl and Ramón work. I used to wait tables there part-time. He was charming and attentive. I guess you have to be if you need to have a lot of women in your life. We dated for about three months before I found out that I was merely his weekday amusement. It turned out that I was just a little fling for him. It was just about a year ago at this time that he informed me he wanted to break things off and hoped there were no bad feelings. Then he brought one of his weekend girls to the restaurant for dinner—just to drive home his point."

"The jerk," Zach said.

"It helped when Daryl spilled red wine on her dress." It also helped that Zach had taken her hand in his.

"Remind me to congratulate Daryl."

"You can cross Boyd the bum off your list. Believe me, he hasn't given me a thought since he dumped me. I was never that important to him."

When he said nothing, merely raised her hand to his lips, something started to flutter in her stomach. It was the same feeling she'd experienced at the restaurant when Zach had mentioned to Daryl that she'd be staying with him at his apartment.

Not fear. It was much different than the iciness that had been rolling around inside of her from the moment that she'd seen her apartment door slightly ajar.

It wasn't nerves she was feeling either because it was nothing like the butterflies that whammed around inside of her when she went to the dentist. No, she was almost positive that the quick skip of her heart she experienced whenever she pictured herself alone with Zach in his apartment was anticipation.

"About staying in your apartment..." She paused as the taxi careened around a corner into Central Park and her hand slipped from Zach's. "It's not necessary. My roommates can keep an eye on me."

"Yes."

The short December day had ended. Even when a streetlight briefly illuminated his features, it was impossible to tell what he was thinking. But he'd agreed with her. She should be feeling relief, not disappointment. Beyond him through the window, she could see the Tavern on the Green lit up like a fairy-tale castle.

There was always a midnight, said the warning voice in the back of her mind.

"Yes what?" she asked.

"Yes, you have two roommates who can keep an eye on you. But they don't get home from work until almost two in the morning. I promised Detective Perez that I would personally keep an eye on you."

Chelsea clasped her hands tightly together in her lap. What in the world was the matter with her? She wanted to go to Zach McDaniels's apartment, to be alone with him. There was a part of her that had wanted that from the first time that he'd kissed her. The heat that shot through her every time she pictured being alone with him, kissing him again, was...desire. Giving in to it would be the worst possible thing that either one of them could do.

"I don't think that going to your apartment would be the smartest idea," she said.

"No."

Chelsea felt her heart sink to her stomach. "Then it's settled."

He turned to her then. "Chelsea, you're staying with me until we find out who's responsible for the threats."

It was joy she was feeling now, wild and free. It was ridiculous and it was wrong and it was absolutely wonderful.

"Ramón and Daryl will be staying at my place too, until your landlord fixes the door and beefs up the security system. I have three guest rooms, plenty of space for everyone. That way all of us will have our eyes on you."

Chelsea stared at him while her heart plummeted right down to her toes.

"I thought you'd feel more comfortable so I made the arrangements with Daryl when we stopped by the restaurant. He has a key."

"You think of everything." Everything except what she'd been thinking. And wanting.

CHELSEA STARED at herself in the small mirror that graced the executive bathroom in Zach's office. Studying her reflection only confirmed what she knew already. She had a straight nose, okay mouth, flyaway hair and fairly plain features.

No one would ever mistake her for a beauty and until this very minute she'd never aspired to be one.

She'd had a different kind of a dream.

Zach McDaniels was mixing her all up. Turning, she

paced the small distance to the shower, then whirled and walked to the door. She wanted him in spite of the fact that he was a total mistake—a heartbreaker, everything her mother had ever warned her against in a man.

In the plus column, he wasn't a bum. A bum didn't offer to take you and your roommates into his home. She might prefer that Zach wanted to carry her off alone to his apartment, but she couldn't deny that his willingness to provide shelter for her roommates was sweet.

She paced to the shower and back to the door. On the minus side, he didn't seem to want her.

And that was a big minus—a real sticking point.

For the past half hour since they'd arrived at his office he'd either been on the phone or sitting at his conference table totally absorbed in the page proofs for the next issue of the magazine. He seemed to have forgotten all about her.

Turning, she walked back to the mirror and studied her reflection again. The truth was she was totally forgettable. All her life men had walked away from her and never given her another thought. Her father had been the first, but certainly not the last. Boyd the bum had only been the most recent in a string of men who'd forgotten her. There'd been Jimmy, the boy who'd given her her first—rather sloppy and disgusting—kiss.

She turned away from the mirror and paced to the door again. It wouldn't do to go through a litany of all of them. It was simply too depressing. Once this business with the threats was over and her articles had all been written and printed, Zach would walk away and forget her, too.

Unless she did something about it...

Stopping short on her path to the shower, she glanced down at the skirt. Could she use it? There were times when she was sure it had worked on Zach.

It was only recently that it hadn't. Could it be losing its power? Quickly, she pressed a hand to the bubble of panic that was blossoming in her stomach. Perhaps, the staples and the tape had weakened it.

Unfastening it at the waist, she pulled down the zipper, then wiggled it down her legs. When she picked it up, she heard two staples ping against the tile floor. Carefully hanging it over the towel rack, she ran her hand down it and rubbed the hem between her fingers.

It looked just the way she felt herself—limp and tired. She didn't see any trace of that shininess that she'd glimpsed when Torrie had tossed it high in the air at the wedding. Moving back, she let the light over the mirror hit it straight on.

Nothing. It looked like an ordinary, basic black skirt.

She sank down onto the toilet and studied it. A few hours ago, she'd been worried that the skirt was working too well on Zach—that he'd never be attracted to her just for herself. Now she was worried that it wasn't working at all. Suddenly, the humor of the situation struck her and she began to laugh.

The sudden knock on the door had her covering her mouth with her hand.

"Are you all right in there?"

She spread her fingers enough to say, "Fine. I'm fine." Then she clamped them shut over her lips to smother a fresh burst of giggles. Clenching her other hand into a fist, she dug her nails into the palm of her hand and took deep breaths. She had to get control.

Control. She flew up off the toilet seat. That was it. Whirling, she began to pace again. Zach had a thing about it. He didn't want to want her. He didn't even like it. She was just going to have to figure out a way to break through that tight control he had.

Frowning, she studied the skirt again. Surely, it hadn't lost its power entirely. Miranda had sworn that it had worked on Harrison Marsh. Maybe there was a way to revive it. Taking it off the rack, she gave it a little shake. More staples pinged against the tiles and a strip of tape floated to the floor. But when she held it to the light, there still wasn't even the glimmer of a shine.

Moonlight, she thought suddenly. Perhaps that was the key. There'd been a full moon in the sky when they'd entered the building.

As the last piece of tape hit the floor, a thought struck her. How in the world was she going to keep the thing on?

9

ZACH PACED to the bathroom door again. She'd been in there forever. He had his hand raised to knock when he heard the low sound—a moan?

He rapped on the door. "Chelsea?"

"I'm...fine."

She didn't sound fine. She sounded upset. Hell, she had a right to be. Every time he thought of what might have happened if she'd been in her apartment, if she hadn't had the sense to run, fear and a sense of help-lessness twisted in his gut. His hand was reaching for the knob when he caught himself.

She was safe. That was the important thing. If she was upset, crying, and he opened the door right now, he would take her into his arms. And once he touched her...

He wouldn't be able to stop there. Turning, he made himself walk to the window, as far away from the bath-room door as he could get. The sky was clear enough to reveal a few stars—he counted five, one brighter than the others.

Keep her safe. The moment he'd made the wish in his mind, he frowned. He hadn't wished on a star in years. Not since he'd learned that wishes didn't come true.

Shifting his attention to the moon, he saw that it was huge and so bright that it nearly made him blink.

You'll never let her go...

He didn't want to let Chelsea go. The realization streamed through him, leaving him stunned. He wanted to take care of her and protect her. He had from the first moment that he'd seen her.

He drew in a deep breath and let it out. All the more reason to stick to his plan. He wasn't going to touch Chelsea again until whoever had destroyed her apartment was behind bars. How could he when he might be responsible for what had happened?

She might not believe that Carter was behind it, but he wouldn't rest easy on that score until he could have it checked out. What if it had been his brother?

A sudden noise from the bathroom had him whirling around and sprinting to the door. Grabbing the handle, he yanked it open and saw Chelsea standing there, clutching the skirt in front of her, her eyes bright with tears.

"Chels." A wave of helplessness washed over him and he was reaching for her when she giggled.

"What is so funny?" he demanded, dropping his hands and struggling to get his system to level.

"This." She waved the skirt like a flag in front of her. He heard two sharp pings, then watched her bend over as a fresh wave of giggles erupted. "Whatever magic Daryl worked with this skirt is totally neutralized. The clock has struck twelve and I'm reduced to rags."

He was trying to make some sense out of what she

was saying when she tucked the skirt over the towel rack and his throat went dry as dust.

"I can't wear the skirt."

He tried to nod intelligently, but he was having trouble separating sounds into words.

"Just when I had plans for it."

"Right." His gaze and his mind were focused totally on her legs. The neat little blazer she wore only skimmed the very tops of her thighs. It no longer made him think of a school uniform.

"Do you have any suggestions about what I should do?"

Several tumbled into his mind, but one was foremost—he couldn't seem to push it away. It would be so easy to lift her to the edge of the vanity. Within seconds, he could slide her thighs apart and eliminate any barriers. Then with her legs wrapped around him, he would begin to move....

He heard a roaring in his ears, his own pulse. More than anything, he wanted to step forward and make the fantasy he'd conjured up in his mind a reality.

But if he did, he would shatter his resolution into a thousand pieces. Taking a quick step back from the doorway, he shoved his hands into his pockets. "You'd better put that skirt back on. When you're decent, we'll talk."

DECENT! CHELSEA frowned at the door Zach had closed behind him. So that was his plan—she was to put her skirt back on so she'd be decent and then they'd talk.

She shot a glance at the skirt. If she put it back on, she'd be decent all right. The hem would hit her at midcalf—not exactly the look she was going for.

Still, if she was going to derail his plan and replace it with one of her own, she was going to need all the help she could get. A man-magnet skirt—even if it had been weakened by staples and tape—could not be ignored.

Reaching for the skirt, she pulled it on, hiking the waistband up to her chest. Then she carefully buttoned her blazer over it and glanced at her reflection in the full-length mirror that hung from one wall.

The big minus was she looked like a cross between a bag lady and the poor little match girl.

Maybe the skirt wasn't as pooped out as it looked. She turned sideways. And maybe it was.

Eyes narrowed, she faced her reflection. Either way, what did she have to lose? If Zach McDaniels intended to walk away from her, she might only have this one night. She wouldn't have anything at all if she stayed in the bathroom all night.

As she turned and walked toward the door, she felt the waistband of the skirt start to slip. Suddenly a plan began to take shape in her mind. Maybe she could find a way for the skirt to help her after all. Smiling, she reached for the knob. With any luck at all, she probably wouldn't be wearing it for very long.

The office was dark except for the small pool of light falling on the conference table. It took her a moment to locate Zach at the window. His back was to her, one hand was fisted on his hip, the other holding his cell phone to his ear. Beyond him, a full moon shone brightly above the sweep of the New York skyline.

"What do you mean you can't locate this..." Zach paused long enough to glance at the card he held in his hand "...Sam Romano?"

He wasn't even looking at her, much less thinking about her. Chelsea made herself walk forward. The skirt dropped another inch.

"Yes, I know he's supposed to meet me at my office at seven-thirty, but something's come up—an emergency." Pausing again, Zach sighed. "Doesn't he have a cell phone or a beeper that you could reach him on?"

There was a brief silence before Zach spoke again. "I see. Yes, I'll expect to see him at seven-thirty then."

Chelsea cleared her throat. "I'm decent." Only because the damn skirt had stopped dropping right at her waist.

Zach didn't even glance her way. Propping one forearm against the window, he gazed down into the street. "I was hoping to move our appointment with the security expert up. That way he could get started, take you back to my apartment and you could get some rest."

"What about you?" Chelsea asked, moving closer.

"I have work to catch up on. I'll be staying here tonight. Mr. Romano will be arranging twenty-four hour protection for you, so you'll be safe."

For a moment, Chelsea said nothing. Zach's message

was pretty clear. He was going to make sure she was taken care of—just not by him. It was a message she'd been given before—by her father. This time she tried to ignore the wave of rejection washing over her. An infant was hardly in a position to change the mind of a reluctant parent. But she wasn't an infant anymore. This time, even if she couldn't change Zach's mind, she'd have a memory of this one night.

Dropping her left hand, she grabbed a fistful of the fabric of the skirt and tugged hard. Then she repeated the same procedure with her right hand, wiggling her hips as she did so. But her blazer was doing too good a job of holding the skirt in place. And Zach seemed altogether fascinated by the scene outside the window. While she gave the skirt another sharp tug, she followed the direction of his gaze.

A Christmas fantasy, she thought as she gazed down at the holiday scene in progress at Rockefeller Center. The tree sparkled with hundreds of lights while skaters blurred together into a rainbow of color as they whirled on the ice rink.

"For a man who claims not to like Christmas, you sure seem fascinated by that picture-postcard scene."

Zach blinked. The truth was he hadn't been looking at the scene below. From the moment she'd joined him at the window, all he'd been able to see was her reflection in the glass. She looked so pale—like an ethereal creature of the moonlight. Someone who couldn't be touched or captured. But the woman standing beside him was real. He could touch her, hold her. In spite of all his resolution, all he could think of was reaching out and doing just that. Fisting his hands, he shoved them into his pockets and said, "I don't like Christmas."

"Okay then." She began unfastening the buttons of her blazer. "You know what they say?" Slipping out of it, she dropped it to the floor.

"What?"

"The best way to get rid of a bad memory is to replace it with a new one." She pulled the button free at her waist.

"Chelsea, what are you doing?"

She shot him one look. Green fire, he thought as he backed to the far side of his desk.

"If you have to ask, I'm not doing it right." She jerked at the zipper. "And this skirt is not helping one bit. It's supposed to draw you like a magnet, and it's having the same effect on you as insect repellent."

Moonlight pooled around her as she moved toward him. For a moment, the skirt seemed to catch the light and glow. Then it once more became transparent and Zach felt his blood begin to pound.

She jerked again at the zipper. Backing away, Zach shook his head to clear it. "You don't want to do that."

"Oh, yes I do," she said, gritting her teeth. This time when she yanked, the zipper opened.

Zach shook his head again. As if it were a signal, the skirt began to inch its way down her hips.

He moved behind a chair; she circled around it, stalking him. His mouth dry as dust, Zach watched the skirt slip lower. "This could be a big mistake."

"Yeah, I know," she said as she gave the waistband a final push and sent it slithering down her legs. "But the thing about mistakes is you never know for sure until you've made them."

He stopped when he backed into the desk. She was still talking as she moved toward him, but he couldn't hear her over the drumming of his heartbeat, couldn't think over her scent swirling through him.

"Now, it's just me," she said as she raised her hands and rested them on his cheeks. "Don't you want me?"

"Chels, I've never wanted anyone more. But you haven't thought this through. I don't want to hurt you."

"What do you think I've been doing in the bathroom? I already figured all the pluses and the minuses." Her hands slid down his neck to unknot his tie. His knees weakened and he sat on the edge of the desk, gripping it hard with his hands. Slowly, she pulled the tie free and tossed it aside. The gesture made the first rip in his restraint.

"I'll skip the minuses. There're way too many," she said, rising on her toes until she could brush her lips against his. "And there's only one plus. This."

It was enough. More than enough, Zach thought as she deepened the kiss and her flavor streamed through him.

"You're irresistible," he murmured against her mouth as he lifted his hands to grip her wrists. Should he have known how free it would feel to give in? If she kept touching him, kissing him, he was going to lose whatever control he had left and take her right on top of his desk.

"Really?" With a quick smile, she freed her hands and went to work on his buttons, slipping them free one at a time. She was pulling his belt off by the time he managed to capture them again.

"I hope your zipper doesn't stick."

He smiled then. "It won't. But I want to take this slow and easy. I can't if you keep touching me."

When she met his eyes, he saw the mischief and the hint of a laugh in hers. "Hard and fast has its pluses. Besides, you can always get it right the second time."

He laughed then. Was he ever going to be able to guess what she'd do or say next? Raising one of her hands, he kissed the veins on the inside of her wrist and felt her pulse scramble, watched her eyes darken. "I'll get it right this time."

"Want to bet?"

The challenge was in her eyes, but her voice had become breathy and she was no longer trying to pull free. Slowly, he raised her other hand and pressed his lips to her palm. "Chels, one thing I need to know—about protection?"

"I'm taking the Pill."

Keeping her hand tightly clasped in his, he leaned forward to press his mouth against her ear. "In that case, perhaps I should point out the minuses of hard and fast," he said.

"You could show me."

"It's all flash and fire. There's no time to imagine, to

wonder what I'll do, where I'll touch you next." The moment she trembled, he drew back.

In the moonlight, her skin had the cool delicate look of porcelain. But it was warm as he brushed just the tips of his fingers along her cheekbone, then tucked a strand of hair behind her ear. "I've waited so long to touch you. I don't want to rush." He ran one finger along her bottom lip. It was warm, moist. There was a pulse at her throat. He traced a path over it and felt it push against his skin. Once more, he felt her tremble and he clamped down on the needs that threatened to boil up like steam in a geyser.

"I want you to think about what it's going to be like." Barely touching her he slipped her buttons free and eased her blouse down her arms. "Imagine exactly what it's going to feel like when my mouth is here." He traced the lace edge at the top of her camisole, then lowered his fingers to graze the tip of her breast. "And here."

When he pressed his mouth to her throat, Chelsea felt her knees turn to water. The scrape of his teeth at her collarbone sent a bolt of heat to her core.

"Did you know that your flavor changes when your skin heats?"

"Mmmmmm." It was the only response she could manage. Her head felt heavy, her arms weighted down as he slipped the strap of her camisole off one shoulder and then the other. Her skin burned as he drew it slowly down to her waist and over her hips. Reality blurred, giving way to the images he created with his words—words he whispered in her ear, telling her where he would touch her next even as his hands and mouth fulfilled his promises.

"Here," he murmured as his fingers traced a slow path down her bare skin to her waist and then below.

She wanted more. It seemed she had waited all her life for the press of those hard, lean hands on her skin. It was the one thought that seemed to filter its way through the sensations that swept over her, each one more vivid than the last. His touch wasn't so gentle now. She could feel hunger in the press of his fingers on her thigh. She could taste desperation when his mouth covered hers.

"Tell me what you want," he whispered against her lips.

"You," she managed. "Please." She was dimly aware of the scratch of carpet against her back, though she had no idea that he'd pulled her to the floor. Then his hand was moving lower, his fingers tracing the edge of her panties, slipping beneath the band to draw them down the length of her legs.

"Soon," Zach promised. To himself and to her. The fire that was raging inside of him, that he'd managed to bank for so long, was threatening to break free. It took all of his strength and control to lever himself up, but he wanted to see her eyes. He had to watch her face as he slipped his fingers into her heat.

She arched once, then again and again. Each movement had his blood pounding, his need doubling. He'd wanted to see her this way, trapped in the pleasure that he could bring her. He wanted her, only her.

You'll never let her go…

The words swirled through his mind as he watched stunned pleasure flood her cheeks and cloud her eyes. Then he gathered her close, holding her tightly as the shudders raced through her.

His own needs tearing through him, he settled his body over her and laced his fingers with hers. Inches away, he stared into her eyes and saw only himself, trapped in green fire. For a moment he didn't move. He'd never wanted a woman more. He'd never needed anyone like this. Even as he plunged into her heat, he was aware that a barrier that he had built deep within himself was crumbling a little each time he moved, each time she moved with him. Then he stopped thinking. He was aware of only her and the waves of sensations she could bring him. Heat. Light. Wind. They all seemed to pull at him as they moved together—faster, higher. But it was the sound of his name on her lips that shot him over the edge. Helpless, he poured himself into her.

10

AFTERWARD, when he could think and breathe again, Zach rolled over but kept Chelsea with him, cradling her against his chest. It was only then that he became fully aware that they were lying half under his desk. The office was dark and quiet. He could feel the beat of her heart against his and the movement of her breath on his skin each time she exhaled. It occurred to him that he could have held her just like that for a very long time.

He had no idea whether or not she felt the same way. Things had happened so fast between them. Good grief, he'd known her for less than a week. They hadn't even gone out on a date. And he'd taken her on the floor of his office. It wasn't his usual style with women. Even as he tried to think of something to say, she reached out and ran her fingers along the leg of his desk chair. She was thinking of something else entirely.

"A penny for your thoughts," he said.

"I was just thinking that I'm still not sure."

Zach frowned. "Not sure of what?"

She rose up then, propping her forearms across his

chest and meeting his eyes. "For a penny, that's all you're going to get."

The laugh broke free before he could prevent it. He tightened his arms around her in a quick hug. "Okay, I'm in for a quarter."

"Wow! Big spender!"

His eyes narrowed. "How about a buck?"

Biting her tongue, she considered then said, "I'm not sure which is better. Slow and easy or fast and hard. As far as I can see, the pluses and minuses are pretty well balanced."

His brows shot up. "Maybe we should try again?"

"My thought exactly."

He moved his hands to cup her face, holding it still so that she had to meet his eyes. "We'll do that right after you tell me what you were really thinking a few minutes ago while you were touching the chair."

She studied him for a minute. "It was silly really. I was just thinking how I had pictured myself sitting in this chair behind this desk, but I never imagined I'd end up practically underneath it like this."

"Are you sorry?"

She smiled slowly. "Are you kidding? As I recall, this was pretty much my idea. I had to work very hard to seduce you. I should be asking you if you're sorry?"

"No."

"Right answer. Otherwise, I might have had to do you a grave bodily injury."

His brows shot up. "Really?"

Before he could stop her, she made a grab for his ear and gave it a quick, hard twist.

"Ouch."

"That's just a sample. I can do much worse."

He grinned at her, but when she started to roll off of him, he held her in place. "You said you pictured yourself in *this* chair? Do you want to run *Metropolitan?*"

"No. I want to be a features editor like Esme Sinclair. I've admired her for the longest time, ever since I first wanted to write for magazines. She even visited my college once and spoke to all the journalism majors. She was sitting behind this desk when I first met with her."

"She must have moved in here while my father was sick." He glanced at the chair. "It's funny that you and I have both wanted to sit in that particular chair. Maybe we have more in common than we think."

"You never sit in it," Chelsea said.

"Of course, I do."

"I've never seen you. You're always sitting on the edge of the desk or over at the conference table. Or you're walking around talking on the phone."

She was right. He did avoid actually sitting in the chair. "I made my mother cry the last time I sat in it." Where had that come from, he wondered the moment that he'd spoken the words aloud. He never talked about his mother. Not to anyone.

"How did you make her cry?" Chelsea asked.

Perhaps it was the way she looked at him, but Zach found himself telling her what had happened that day when he was five and he'd made the mistake of using his father's pen.

"You didn't make her cry. Your father did when he yelled at you for something that wasn't your fault," Chelsea said in a very matter-of-fact tone when he'd finished. Then very slowly, she lowered her mouth to his and kissed him.

It was different. There was a sweetness in the kiss that he hadn't felt before.

She was the one who drew back first. "C'mon. I have an idea."

Before he could stop her, she had rolled off of him and had risen to her feet. Then reaching down, she grabbed his hand and tugged. "It's supposed to help to erase a bad memory if you replace it with a good one. Have you ever made love in a chair?

"You're kidding."

"No, I'm absolutely serious. Have you?"

"I'm going to take the fifth on that one."

"Oh. That means yes, right?"

"Chelsea," he began.

"It's good that one of us has some expertise here because I've never—" She stopped short to frown at the chair, tilting her head to one side. "I suppose that there are various positions we could take?"

"Several come to mind. Let me get this straight. You want me to make love to you in that chair?"

"By George, I think you've got it!"

"Yeah, it takes me a while sometimes." When she took his arms to push him into the chair, he scooped her up by the waist and carried her with him. Once seated, he gripped her hips and positioned her so that she was straddling him.

"Oh," she said again as he pushed himself into her. "Ohhh."

"Is this what you had in mind?"

"Mmmm, even better. Once you get it, you're really quite good."

"Chels." He was chuckling as he drew her face close so that he could nip her ear. "If you continue to make me laugh, you may not get the results you're looking for."

"Then I'll get serious," she murmured as she took his mouth with hers.

She got very serious. And so did he.

"THAT'S ABOUT IT, Romano," Zach said, then turned to Chelsea. "Unless you have anything to add?"

Chelsea shook her head. Sam Romano the security consultant Zach had hired was seated across the conference table from her. The lean, dark-haired man wore a well-tailored suit and had been taking copious notes since he'd arrived. And Chelsea was trying to put her finger on the reason she sensed a certain tension between the two men.

Maybe it was because they were so much alike—both tall and dark and strikingly handsome. Each had charm to burn, although Sam Romano's particular brand was much more overt—from the laugh that seemed to be perpetually present in his dark brown eyes to his easy tone and engaging grin. Chelsea had a hunch that all of his clients must trust him and if they were female they probably fell a little bit in love with him right from that first handshake.

"What I need from your firm is a bodyguard for Chelsea," Zach said.

Sam stopped writing for a moment and glanced up from his notebook. "I agree. I'll be on the job first thing in the morning."

"You?" Zach asked, then frowned. "I was assuming that your firm had people who specialized in providing personal protection. You don't look like a bodyguard."

Sam grinned at him. "That's why I make a good one. Before I went to work for Sterling Security, I worked as a private investigator in my cousin's firm. When there's a job that calls for street experience, Sterling usually turns it over to me."

Zach's frown didn't fade as he studied Sam for a moment. Then he reached over to cover Chelsea's hand with his. "As long as you understand that Ms. Brockway's welfare is very important to me. She'll be staying with me at my apartment until this matter concerning her safety is resolved. Do we understand each other?"

Zach was staking out a claim, Chelsea realized. No wonder she'd sensed tension between the two men. Before she could sort out the feelings moving through her—pleasure, annoyance—Sam nodded. "I understand you perfectly. Between us, I think we can watch over Ms. Brockway. The problem is that she might not be the only one in danger."

"What do you mean?" Zach asked.

Sam flipped through his notes. "The car you mentioned—the one that nearly ran you down near Rockefeller Center. It would have hit you both, right? And you received a threatening note this morning reminding you of it. This person may have a grudge against you and Ms. Brockway could just be an innocent bystander."

Trying to ignore the quick spurt of fear shooting through her, Chelsea laced her fingers with Zach's. "Sam's right. You need a bodyguard, too."

"Maybe not." Zach met Sam's eyes squarely. "I'm going to tell you something that I didn't tell the police. I think it might have been my brother who's sending the notes. He might be behind the phone calls, too. He wants me to resign from my job here at the magazine. But I'm not in any personal danger. I don't believe he'd hurt Chelsea either. He'd only want to scare her."

"Unless he was behind the wheel of that car," Sam said. "But let's suppose, for the moment, that it's not your brother. As I understand it, you've just stepped in as editor of *Metropolitan* and you intend to make a lot of changes. Some people might resent that and want to see you fail."

"Yes, I suppose so." Pausing, Zach frowned. "But if it's someone here at the magazine who has something against me, why would they take it out on Ms. Brock-way? I don't see the connection."

Sam leaned forward. "You've signed her to a con-tract. If her articles do well for the magazine, that would be a feather in your cap. Right?"

Zach nodded. "I suppose."

"Who here at the magazine would like to see you fail?" Sam asked.

"Bill Anderson and Hal Davidson would head the list," Zach said. "Then you can add the rest of my edi-torial staff."

Sam flipped to a fresh page in his notebook. "Tell me about them."

By the time Zach had finished, Sam was frowning thoughtfully. "I'll have them checked out. The fact that Christmas is just days away will slow the process down a little."

"You got any hunches?" Zach asked.

Sam shook his head. "It's too soon. It could be that we've got two different things going on here. On the one hand, there are some people who are very, shall we say, *disgruntled* about your new position as editor of *Metropolitan*. Some even want you to step down. Then there are others who are upset about the kind of arti-cles that Ms. Brockway is writing for the magazine so they want to put a stop to that."

"You're saying there might be more than one person behind all this?" Chelsea asked.

"Bingo," Sam said. "Or it could be just one person— say your ex-boyfriend. If he's the kind of looney tune that Detective Perez had in mind." He shifted his gaze to Zach. "I'll check him out. And your brother, too."

Zach's gaze narrowed. "You think both of them could be involved?"

"What I think is that we've got some puzzle pieces. We won't know how they all fit together until we get some more. In the meantime, I think that both of you need protection." He flipped to a new page in his notebook. "It's the weekend so it would help if you could provide me with an itinerary of your plans for the next two days."

"Tomorrow, I'm going to the MOMA, the skating rink at Rockefeller Center and then—"

"You're going to have to change your plans," Zach said turning to Sam. "Tell her it's too dangerous."

Sam's grin flashed quick and easy as he held up both hands, palms out. "I have this rule not to get involved in domestic disputes. It dates back to my P.I. days."

Chelsea wanted to hug him, but she stifled the impulse and smiled at him instead. "Thank you very much, Sam." She turned to Zach. "You're determined to print the articles. That means I have to write them. The sooner I do, the sooner this will be over."

She was right. He turned to Sam. "Can you protect her?"

"I have a pair of skates I haven't used in a few years," Sam said. "I used to be fairly competent on the ice. If someone is after one or the both of you, we're not going to lure them out if you hole up for the weekend."

"I'll be coming along, too," Zach said.

"Great," Sam said, his grin widening. "That'll make it real simple to protect you."

"YOU CAN'T SKATE with me," Chelsea said.

Not bothering to glance up, Zach jerked at a knot in the laces of his skate. "We settled this in the taxi. You're not going out on that ice alone."

As far as Chelsea was concerned, the only thing that had been settled in the taxi was that Sam had lost the coin toss deciding who was going to go out on the ice with her. The rest of the ride had been taken up with arguing. But the arguing was better than the wall of silence that Zach had built between them since they'd made love.

When they'd reached his apartment last night, it was as if he'd forgotten that they'd made love together. He'd escorted her politely to one of the guestrooms and told her that they both needed to sleep.

His control was back in place. He'd probably spent the night listing all the pluses and minuses of making love with her again. The minuses clearly had won. They always did when it came to the men in her life.

Fine. She took a deep breath. She would just stick to her own agenda. The focus of her second article was to see how the skirt worked at various New York landmarks. She was ahead of schedule thanks to the fact that they'd been asked to leave the Museum of Modern Art.

From the bench they were sitting on, she could see

that the rink was already crowded with a variety of skaters, from children to older couples, from obvious beginners to a young man who was just coming out of a professional-looking spin. There were definitely some men skating without partners. That was a good sign.

The question was: would the skirt have some effect on them?

Beside her, Zach muttered under his breath as one of his laces broke.

Perhaps the bigger question was: would the man sitting next to her let her put the skirt to a test without interfering again?

Leaning closer to Zach, she said, "I think we need to set up some ground rules here. When you come out on the ice with me, you have to keep your distance and give the skirt a chance to work. No one will come near me if you start lurking too close like you did at the MOMA."

"My *lurking* saved you from being assaulted by a dirty old man."

Her brows shot up. "Funny how the security guard thought that you were the one harassing me. You were the one he asked to leave the museum."

"Yeah, well, he was conveniently looking the other way when that old man started to paw you. All he saw was my reaction."

"You grabbed a helpless old man and pinned him against the wall!"

When Zach straightened from tying his skate, Chelsea became suddenly aware of how close they were—nearly mouth to mouth.

"Chels, come back to the apartment with me."

She could feel the heat of his breath on her lips. The cool reserve that had been in his eyes since they'd left the office last night had vanished. In its place was something hot, dark and reckless. It had her heart fluttering like the snowflakes that had begun to tumble from the sky.

When his hand moved to rest along the side of her throat, she felt her pulse skip, then quicken. She wanted him. It was just that quick, that simple, that elemental.

"Chels—"

There was a part of her that wanted very much to forget what they'd come here to do and go back to Zach's apartment. She was even willing to forget the way that he'd pushed her away.

"What do you say? We could go back and spend the rest of the day—"

He leaned closer to whisper in her ear. Her whole brain began to fog as he described exactly what they could do for the rest of the day. In some part of her mind, she was aware of sounds—someone clearing their throat, a snatch of music escaping briefly from someone's headphones. But she was totally lost in the images that Zach was creating. They were so tempting and it would be so easy... She had to say something, anything, or her body was just going to get up and go with him.

"Excuse me. I was wondering if..."

Zach didn't release Chelsea as he turned. "What do you want?"

The woman, a frazzled looking brunette flanked by two little girls, took a quick step back at Zach's tone. "I wanted to use the bench. My daughters and I need to put on our skates. I thought because your skates are on, we could..."

"Of course you can use the bench," Chelsea said, and the moment that Zach loosened his grip, she stood up.

Zach pulled her back down. "It'll just take us a moment to get out of our skates."

"Get out of our—" Chelsea felt the sensual fog she'd been trapped in finally lift. "No, we can't go yet. I have to skate." She stilled his hands on the laces. Though their faces were close, she didn't look at him. If she did, all her new-found resolve would waver. "We decided all this last night with Sam and again just now in the taxi. I need this research to finish the articles. The sooner I do, the safer we both will be."

Standing, Chelsea smiled at the woman and her two daughters. "Sorry we held you up."

SHE WAS AWAY from him in a flash. Although Zach found it difficult to run after her on skates, it got worse once both of his blades hit the ice. Immediately, he began to wobble. Quickly, he grabbed for the nearby rail to steady himself, and by the time he did, he'd lost sight of Chelsea.

Fighting down a bubble of fear that had already formed in his stomach, he began to swear steadily and silently to himself as he scanned the skaters moving in a wide oval pattern around the rink.

No need to panic. She was on the rink. She would have to skate past him. All he had to do was wait. When he noticed how white his knuckles were on the hand gripping the rail, he concentrated on relaxing his fingers.

Then he spotted her at the far end of the rink, skating as if she didn't have a care in the world. His relief began to war with anger. At her, at himself. She was safe, he reminded himself. They were in a very public place. No one would try anything here. But nothing in the little lecture he was giving himself was having any effect on the urge he had to shake her.

Frowning, he watched the whirling dervish who'd been wowing the crowd skate alongside of her. He had to clamp down tight on his desire to go punch the guy in the face.

No one had ever gotten to him this way. He'd never allowed anyone to chip through the careful control he'd layered around himself. Not until Chelsea.

He'd made an absolute fool of himself at the museum. Not that he was sorry. That old man would think twice before he put his hands on another young woman. But Zach couldn't forget the fact that for the first time in his life, he'd actually seen red. Just thinking about it was enough to have the fury bubbling up again. If Sam hadn't been there, he might have done more than pin that old guy to the wall.

It wasn't just his temper that he seemed to lose control of whenever he was around Chelsea. Although that was troubling enough. The fact was he couldn't stop thinking about making love to her.

Lord knows, he'd tried. At his insistence, she'd spent the night in his apartment, but he'd put her in his guest room, not in his bed. He'd told her it was because he wanted her to get some sleep. And it was partly the truth. They wouldn't have gotten any sleep at all if she'd been in his bed. He'd told himself that he needed to keep some objectivity if he wanted to protect her. But he'd also wanted to prove to himself that he could keep some distance between them.

Well, he'd done that all right. All in all, it was a night that he could be proud of, he thought as disgust rolled around in his belly. He hadn't gotten a wink of sleep and he'd hurt Chelsea. Not that she'd said anything to him. But she'd sensed his withdrawal and no doubt was viewing it as rejection.

"Great work, McDaniels," he muttered to himself as she sailed past without even a glance in his direction. Only the fact that Mr. Show-off was still at her side kept him at the railing. Close up, the young man looked harmless enough, a teenager out to impress an older woman—although, the kid might not realize that Chelsea was older. She looked like a teenager herself, whipping around the ice in that skirt. His gaze was on her skirt when it happened. Mr. Show-off went into a sudden spin and one of his skates caught the back of Chelsea's. She was pitching forward onto the ice when Zach pushed off from the railing.

To offset the fact that his feet immediately sailed out from under him, he lurched forward. Then just as he was about to topple face first into the ice, he jerked his body backward. In a last ditch attempt to find his equilibrium, he flailed his arms in huge circles. Even then, he might have achieved some kind of balance—if he hadn't been struck suddenly from behind. Seconds later he kissed the ice.

11

THE NEXT THING Zach knew he was lying facedown with a huge weight pressing him into the ice.

"Zach, are you all right?"

Twisting around, he saw Chelsea's face first. He managed to take in one good breath before another face blocked hers out. This one was chubby and freckled, framed in a riot of red curls and grinning ear to ear.

"That was a great trick. Will you show me how to do it?" it asked and then burst into a fit of giggles.

"Who are you?" Zach asked as he lifted the owner of the face off of him. He figured the kid was about seven or eight.

"I'm not supposed to talk to strangers," the kid said.

Zach sat up. "This is my friend Chelsea and I'm Zach."

"Hi. Here come my friends."

Zach turned in time to see a kid in a red jacket throw himself down on the ice and skid into his thigh. A blue-jacketed bullet came next, hitting him in the shoulder as a dynamo in black somersaulted over him.

"Joey, Sid and Carl," the redhead said. "I'm Marty."

"Zach," he said, shaking hands with each one, "and my friend Chelsea."

"We already know her," Marty said. "She's the skirt lady we saw at the TV station yesterday. We got her autograph."

As if on signal, another little boy slammed into her and she ended up sitting on the ice next to Zach. "Cub Scouts," she explained. "They were visiting the TV studio yesterday."

"Can I touch the skirt?" Marty asked, crawling across Zach.

"Sure."

At Chelsea's consent, the boy made a grab for the hem. "It's soft." Then lifting it to his nose, he began to sniff it. "It smells like flowers."

Immediately, three other little guys began to sniff the skirt.

"I'm beginning to think this skirt should come with a warning from the Surgeon General," Zach muttered as he pried the first one loose. "That's it guys. Cub Scouts don't sniff ladies' skirts."

"I'm so sorry," said the blond woman skating to a stop next to Chelsea. "I hope they're not bothering you. You were so nice to give them your autograph yesterday. Marty, let the nice lady..." Her voice trailed off as he gaze fell on Zach. "Oh, my heavens. You're the—" She turned to Chelsea. "It's him, isn't it? The *hottie.*"

Making a quick pivot on the ice, she began to wave frantically. "Mary! Bethany! Come over here! It's *him!*"

CHELSEA SCRAMBLED to her feet, then found herself quickly edged aside by the two other women who had crossed the ice with the speed and focused determination of Olympic racers. Within seconds, they had admonished their sons not to race, had Zach on his feet and backed up against the railing, signing autographs.

When he sent her a pleading and desperate glance, she couldn't prevent a smile. He was sweet, she thought. There'd been a gentleness in the way he'd handled little Marty that she hadn't seen before. And he was being so patient with the women. As her gaze was held by his, a warmth moved through her that was totally different from the other feelings that he'd engendered in her.

It struck her then and she had to skate to the railing to keep herself from sitting right down on the ice.

She was in love with Zach McDaniels. Keeping a tight grip on the rail, she turned to stare at him. He was still scribbling on the notebooks the women were pushing at him, but his eyes were on her. Could he tell what she was thinking, she wondered as a sliver of panic skipped up her spine.

Maybe it wasn't too late to nip this in the bud. Quickly, she tried to list the minuses in her mind—all the reasons why Zach McDaniels was the last person in the world she should be in love with. Topping the list was a biggie.

He was not in love with her.

Oh, he might want to have sex with her, but it ended there. She tried to concentrate on this one inescapable fact, but the feelings swirling within her told her that she was sinking fast. That first spurt of panic had given way to something else—something that made her want to go into a spin on the ice that she might not come out of. It made her want to shout and even start singing.

That would clear the rink, she thought with a quick glance around. On the other hand, it would leave her alone with Zach. In her mind, she pictured them alone on the ice, skating toward each other, the music swelling.

The only thing wrong with the picture in her mind was that Zach wouldn't hang around very long—especially if she told him she was falling in love with him.

"I've got to hand it to you. You're one smooth operator."

Chelsea tore her gaze from Zach to find Hal Davidson, the political editor from *Metropolitan*, standing next to her on the ice. "What are you doing here?"

Hal waved a hand at his skates. "Same as you. The rink's open to the public. I just didn't think to invite the boss."

Chelsea studied him for a moment. His smile seemed genuine, but it didn't reach his eyes.

"I didn't invite him," she said. "And it's not what you think. I'm doing research for my next article and Mr. McDaniels insisted on coming along."

"Mr. McDaniels? Surely, you're on a first-name basis with him by now—someone who works as quickly as you do."

In spite of the fact that she was in a public place and perfectly safe, Chelsea felt a sliver of anxiety skip up her spine. It didn't help one bit that Zach was still surrounded by the Cub Scout moms or that she couldn't see any sign of Sam Romano.

"He's usually more careful and more selective about the women he lets himself get involved with."

Chelsea could feel the heat flooding her cheeks, but she managed to keep her voice even. "Since we both came here to skate, I think that's what we should do."

He took her arm as she pushed past him, and he turned up the wattage on his smile. "Look, I didn't mean to insult you. We're two of a kind, you and me. Confidentially, I'm impressed that you convinced McDaniels to honor your contract. And getting yourself on *Good Morning, New York* was a brilliant move. At least I thought it was until yesterday afternoon. But it's backfired."

"I don't know what you're talking about."

Hal frowned. "McDaniels didn't tell you about the bad news we got at the staff meeting yesterday? Three longtime advertisers have canceled their accounts with *Metropolitan*, and they cited your articles as the reason they're leaving. They don't approve of the direction the magazine is obviously going in. By Tuesday, other advertisers will be stumbling over each other trying to jump ship. It's only a matter of time—a very short amount of time—until your boss and perhaps the magazine will be history."

Chelsea lifted her chin. "I wouldn't count on it."

Hal's grip on her arm tightened. "Oh, but I am. And if you're smart, you'll count on it too. I have an offer from *New York Now,* and they want you, too. I told them I could get you. McDaniels should be more than happy to release you from your contract now that he knows those articles are going to be the cause of *Metropolitan's* demise. Think about it. You'll be in a much better bargaining position if you go to them before you're fired by the new editor-in-chief."

Before she could reply, Hal had turned and disappeared smoothly into the throng of skaters now circling the rink.

"Are you all right?"

This time Chelsea was surprised and relieved to find Sam at her elbow. "I'm fine. Better now that you're here. But I thought your plan was to stay off the ice."

"That changed once you got separated from McDaniels. That guy who just left—who was he?"

"Hal Davidson. He's the political editor at *Metropolitan.*"

"Quite a coincidence that he'd turn up skating today, don't you think?" As Sam spoke, she followed Hal's progress as he left the rink and made his way to a bench.

"I don't think it was a coincidence at all." By the time she'd filled in Sam on the offer Hal had made her, Sam was on his cell phone, giving curt orders to someone. "Yeah, I want you to tail him. Let me know where he goes. And call the office, see what we've turned up on him so far."

"You don't think that Hal could be behind everything that's happened, do you?" Chelsea asked.

"I don't think anything yet," Sam said, pocketing his phone. "I learned a long time ago not to jump to any conclusions until all the evidence is in. Speaking of that, I'd like to get you off this rink. You must have gathered all the data you need here."

"So far, with all the interruptions, I've gotten squat."

Sam grinned at her. "You've got to be kidding. Men have been hitting on you since you first got on the ice. First you've got the twirling dervish guy spinning into the railing trying to impress you. Then comes the attack of the Cub Scouts."

Chelsea shook her head. "They're just kids. They saw me on TV yesterday and were fascinated because they think the skirt has special powers. Kids that age are into that kind of Merlin and magic stuff."

Sam threw back his head and laughed. "Sniffing lady's skirts is something guys are into at pretty much any age. From where I was standing, they had some of the smoothest moves I've seen."

Chelsea stared at him. "I never thought about it that way. Maybe I could use it—" She broke off when she saw Zach push his way past his last fan and start toward them. When he started to wobble almost immediately, Chelsea frowned. "He can't skate."

"Yeah. That's another reason I decided to join you on the ice," Sam said.

"Why on earth didn't he just say so? Why did he insist on coming out here with me?"

Sam shot her a glance. "The guy's batty over you."

Chelsea shook her head firmly. "No, he's not."

"Believe me, I saw it happen to my old partner. I know the signs. One of them is you start doing crazy—"

Chelsea never heard the rest of Sam's sentence because she had to get to Zach. Reaching him, she grabbed one of his flailing arms and drew it across her shoulders. "What were you thinking coming out here on the ice? You don't know how to skate."

"I do, too. My mother taught me right here on this rink. It's not something you forget. It's like riding a bike or typing."

Chelsea turned to him then. "How old were you when you learned?"

"Five. What difference does that make? I learned. I know how to skate. I'm just a little rusty."

"If you were only five, I'll bet your skates had double runners on them. That's why you're having trouble."

"What was Hal Davidson talking to you about?" Zach asked.

"I'll make you a deal," Chelsea said. "I'll tell you all about it while I give you a skating lesson."

"I don't need—" Zach began.

"It won't take any time at all. I started skating on runners, too. You just have to make a little transition to single blade skates." Grabbing his hand, she tugged him along. "Push off with your left foot, glide with your right. Then push with your right foot and glide with your left. That's it."

As they completed one full turn around the rink, she filled him in on Hal's offer and he wasn't even thinking about skating or what he was doing with his feet. He was just doing it.

"You've got it," she said. The words were barely out of her mouth when someone smacked into them. She held tight to Zach as the impact sent them both hurtling across the ice. Swerving to avoid other skaters, she was still struggling to keep them both balanced when someone slammed into them again. This time her skates flew out from under her. Her back hit the ice first, then her head. For a moment she lay staring upward watching stars mix with the whirl of snowflakes.

A shout had her rolling over and scrambling to her knees. She saw Sam lying on top of someone on the ice. And Zach was down, too. She could see him, sprawled on the ice, one arm outstretched. Not moving.

For a moment, her heart stopped and she couldn't move either.

Then he stirred, rolling over and levering himself up. She'd started to crawl toward him, had almost closed the distance, when she saw the blood staining the ice.

ZACH THREW his legs over the side of the hospital gurney the moment the doctor stepped out of the room. It had been four hours since they'd arrived at the hospital—four hours since he'd seen Chelsea. They'd wheeled her away first since she'd whacked her head against the ice. His sliced arm had been less of a priority once the bleeding had been stopped.

It was some consolation that the man who'd knifed him was in police custody. Sam had been in contact with the precinct where the man was being held. All he'd been able to find out so far was that the guy had a record. That was when the nurse had shooed Sam out of the room so the doctor could stitch Zach's arm. Dropping to the floor, Zach put his good arm on the gurney to steady himself. He was halfway to the door when the pretty Asian doctor blocked his escape with a wheelchair.

"You can't leave without your limo," she said, waving her hand toward the chair.

If she'd been a man, he could have handled her. But the tiny woman in front of him had bullied and finally bribed him into getting his arm stitched up, so he did not underestimate his opponent. "What did you find out about Chelsea Brockway?"

Her brows shot up. "She's a much better patient than you are."

Zach clamped down on a spurt of temper, only because he was sure it would only delay his escape. Instead, he managed a smile while he glanced at her name tag. Iris Tong. "Dr. Tong. Iris. We had a deal. You got to practice your needlework on my arm and now I intend to find out where you've taken Ms. Brockway." In his attempt to move past her, his elbow brushed the back of the wheelchair and in spite of the anesthetic, pain shot to his shoulder.

The doctor stepped into his path. "Her X rays showed no sign of a concussion. Ms. Brockway is fine. But you won't be if that arm starts bleeding again."

"I want to see her." He started past her again, but she grabbed his good arm.

"If you want to see your Ms. Brockway, get in the chair."

He hesitated.

"I can get you to her faster in the chair because I know where she is. You don't."

He looked at her, almost amused. "You have a lousy bedside manner."

"Yeah." She grinned at him at he settled himself in the chair. "But my patients do what I tell them because I figure out their weak spots. And yours is Ms. Brockway. You're crazy in love with her."

Zach said nothing as she wheeled him down the short hallway. He didn't even speak to Sam when they rolled past him at the nurse's station. All he could think of was that he couldn't be in love with Chelsea. Attraction was one thing—but love? Fear bubbled up. No. It was impossible.

"I'll bet you even smell flowers when there's none around," Dr. Tong said.

"How did you...?"

"I'm a very good doctor."

Zach scanned the waiting room. It took him a moment to spot Chelsea because she was surrounded by men. In some part of his mind he recognized Ramón standing behind her and he registered that two of the others wore green scrubs. But his attention was riveted on the man kneeling on the floor with his head up her skirt! Zach was out of the wheelchair and across the waiting room in two quick strides.

"There," the headless man began. "I think that should—"

Zach grabbed the front of the man's shirt and jerked.

"Zach!" Chelsea blocked his raised fist at the same time that Sam wrapped his arms around his waist from behind.

He was about to shake both of them off when the red mist in front of his eyes cleared enough for him to recognize Daryl and to see that Chelsea had moved in front of her roommate.

"Peace." Daryl plucked a white handkerchief out of his pocket and waved it around Chelsea's shoulder. "I was just doing some damage control with the skirt."

"To hell with the skirt. I wish I'd never seen it," Zach said, then winced as he tried to wrap his bad arm around Chelsea. "You're all right?"

"I'm fine. But your arm's not." She turned to the doctor. "Is it?"

"It should be fine if he can control his impulse to punch people out," Dr. Tong said with a smile. Then she signaled for the two men in scrubs to follow her.

Keeping his good arm around Chelsea, Zach turned to Sam. "Have you learned anything more about the man who knifed me?"

Sam glanced at Daryl and Ramón.

"You can talk in front of them," Zach said.

"The knifer's done it before. One of the detectives on the case thinks he may have been hired."

"That settles it." Zach turned to Chelsea. "We're going back to my apartment and you're going to take off that skirt for good."

"I can't. I'm wearing it to your aunt's ball tonight."

"You're not going."

"Of course, I'm going. You're the one who should stay home."

Zach drew in a deep breath. He wasn't going to win this argument by shouting. "I can't protect you. I thought I could, but I can't." Even as he spoke, he thought of that moment when he'd seen the blood staining the ice and thought it was Chelsea's. Shoving down the panic that was bubbling up all over again, he said, "I won't allow you—the magazine can't allow you to put your life in danger for the sake of a foolish article."

Chelsea stepped back from him. The hurt and anger he saw in her eyes sliced through him, but he didn't reach for her. The only thing he could allow himself to think of was keeping her safe.

"It's *my* life and *my* foolish article," she said. "I'm not the one who was knifed."

But you could have been. It was the image that had been flashing through his mind since they'd left the ice rink. He hadn't been able to stop it.

"The skirt articles are over. *Metropolitan* won't be running the last two."

Chelsea's chin shot up. "Fine."

"You'll stay at my apartment tonight. Sam will be able to protect you there."

"No," Chelsea said, taking another step back from him. "I won't be staying at your apartment."

"Chels—" But when he reached for her, she stepped even further away.

"The super got in touch with Daryl and Ramón. The apartment door's been fixed and a security system has been installed. I'm going with them."

When she turned to walk away, Zach managed to keep from reaching out to her. Instead, he said to Sam. "Take care of her."

"My pleasure."

He grabbed Sam's arm as the man moved past him. "She's mine."

Sam grinned. "Yeah. I can tell. You're acting like a total jerk. That's a sure sign you're crazy about her."

12

Fantasy. Glitz. Glamour. It was everywhere that Chelsea looked. Miranda had worked a miracle, transforming the top floor of the Miramar Hotel into a true Christmas wonderland. Twinkling lights cascaded from the ceiling, and flowers were everywhere, banking the food and drink stations and lining the walls of windows that offered breathtaking views of the Manhattan skyline. It was a treat for the senses—the scent of food mingling with flowers, candlelight gleaming off crystal and silver, violin music mixing with the sound of laughter.

And Chelsea was absolutely miserable. Zach was furious with her. He hadn't spoken to her once since she'd arrived at the ball with Daryl as her date.

Even now, he was seated across from her at Miranda's table just as far away as he could get.

Of course, he'd been talking to board members. She'd been busy, too. Her feet hurt from dancing with all the men Miranda had introduced her to. She'd even managed a dance with Sam Romano. He'd assured her that every possible precaution was being taken to protect Zach. But not even his reassurance had melted the tight fist of fear that had settled in her stomach ever since she'd seen Zach's blood on the ice. If the knifer's aim had been just a bit more accurate...

No, she wasn't going to dwell on that. But did Zach think that while his life was in danger, she was just going to sit at his apartment and wait? Not bloody likely! Not when she could keep an eye on him herself.

When she realized she was looking at Zach again, she tried to look away and couldn't. Thousands of little champagne bubbles bumped against her heart. He was so reserved, so aloof, so controlled. The complete opposite of her. She could probably stare at him all evening like some lovesick puppy and he wouldn't so much as glance her way. If she made the first move and approached him he might merely ignore her and walk away.

Tearing her gaze away from him, she tried to gather her thoughts. She'd come here to gather data for her article and that's what she was going to do. Miranda had been so helpful, introducing her to several celebrities, including a rap star who'd not only complimented her on her dress, but had even asked her to dance. She could already imagine how she was going to write that up.

She'd danced with James McCarthy, the host of *Good Morning, New York*. He'd been very sweet, thanking her again for appearing on his show and raving about the spike in his ratings. He'd even very thoughtfully straightened the strap that had become twisted on her shoulder and offered to escort her out on one of the balconies for a breath of fresh air. They'd been stepping through the French doors when Miranda had interrupted and dragged her away.

The skirt was clearly a success. Daryl had outdone himself. The black sequined top he'd designed had thin straps over the shoulders and fit snugly to the waist. But the real miracle he'd worked had been on the skirt itself. Somehow, with tape, staples and a little bit of smoke and mirrors, he'd fixed it so that it looked like it had been made to go with the top.

When Miranda had introduced her to three of the board members' wives, they'd asked for the name of her designer. Luckily, she'd been able to introduce them to Daryl. Because *he* was her date, not Zach.

She pressed a hand against her heart just as the champagne bubbles bombarded it again.

"Your boss is looking daggers at me, too," Daryl complained in a low tone as he pantomimed pulling one out of his arm and tossed it on the floor.

"I don't want to talk about him," she said.

Miranda leaned close to Chelsea. "I haven't had this much fun in years. Zach is clearly taken with you."

"He likes me about as much as he likes poison ivy."

"You didn't see his face when James McCarthy was fiddling with your dress. I won't tell you what he threatened to do if I didn't drag you away from him. He rarely lets a woman—or anyone else for that matter—get under his skin. And you got him to go skating at Rockefeller Center. He hasn't skated since he was five."

"Why not? He really does know how," Chelsea said.

"He just needed to get the feel of doing it on a single blade."

Miranda looked at her. "He didn't tell you."

"Tell me what?"

"He was skating with his mother on Christmas Eve when she collapsed. They rushed her to the hospital, but it was too late. Her heart had always been weak. The doctors had warned her not to have children. I think deep down my brother blamed Zach for Mary's death."

Chelsea couldn't prevent herself from looking at Zach then. She didn't see the man who'd rejected her that afternoon. Nor did she see the cool, aloof man who was ignoring her now. Instead, she saw the little boy who'd been skating when he'd lost his mother.

And yet, he'd gone with her onto the ice. Hope was blooming in her heart when his gaze met hers. Cold, blue ice was what she saw. It nearly made her teeth chatter. It definitely made her spine stiffen.

"I'd like to dance with someone," she said.

"At your service," Daryl said.

"No offense, Daryl, but we've established that the skirt doesn't work on you. I need to do my job and finish gathering data."

Miranda scanned the dance floor. "Let's see if we can kill two birds with one stone. Ah," she said, rising and drawing Chelsea with her. "I have just the person. Have you met Zach's brother?"

"Briefly," Chelsea said. "Our meeting didn't go well."

Miranda took her arm and urged her toward the dance floor. "We have him at a disadvantage now. He's in public and he can't afford a scene."

"He's still not going to want to dance with me."

Miranda shot her a grin. "Let's see if the skirt can take on a challenge, shall we?"

ZACH WANTED to throttle her. He wanted to grab her and drag her away to safety. But he couldn't go near her. Keeping his distance was the only way he could keep her safe. It was the only strategy that he and Sam could come up with once Daryl had called to warn them that Chelsea was determined to come to the ball and that he was coming with her. Of course, Zach should have expected it. Why had he thought even for a moment that she would do the sensible thing and stay home where she would be safe? He owed Daryl for offering to escort her.

Unclenching his hands, Zach rose from the table and moved toward one of the drink stations so that he could keep Chelsea in sight. It would have been easier if they were any closer to figuring out who was behind the threats, but they weren't. So far all Sam had been able to come up with was that the police had eliminated Boyd Carter because he had been out of the country skiing for two weeks.

That left Jerry at the head of the suspect list.

As he ordered a drink, he scanned the room and saw that he wasn't the only one who had moved closer to

Chelsea. Both Daryl and Sam had shifted to spots near the edge of the dance floor.

Taking the drink from the bartender, Zach nearly let it slip through his fingers as his aunt tapped his brother on the shoulder. He'd taken two steps toward the dance floor before Daryl stepped into his path. "I have two messages. But I want to make sure you're not going to kill the messenger."

"Go ahead," Zach said.

"Miranda wants Chelsea to work a little magic on your brother and I'll cut in at the first sign of any trouble."

Zach studied him for a moment. "I want to thank you for bringing her tonight."

"No problem. After seeing the apartment, I wouldn't have let her come alone. Ramón couldn't possibly get away from the restaurant or he'd be here, too."

Zach's gaze narrowed as he studied Daryl's face. "What about you? They can't have been happy when you told them you weren't coming in. Are you going to have a job after tonight?"

Daryl grinned at him. "Who cares? After seeing Chelsea, four of your board members' wives want me to design them outfits and several others want replicas of her skirt. One of them gave the card of a buyer at Bloomingdale's and told me to use her name."

"It sounds to me like you need a financial backer. On Wednesday, why don't you come to my office. We'll—"

"I'm sorry." Miranda was slightly out of breath as she reached them. "I need to borrow Daryl."

Zach watched them thread their way through the other couples on the dance floor until they were close to Jerry and Chelsea. Then he took a long swallow of his scotch.

In another hour it would be midnight and he'd nearly finished what his aunt had mapped out for him to do. The only board member he hadn't spoken to yet was Harrison Marsh, the president. When Chelsea had danced with him, the man who was known for his poker-faced sobriety had laughed three times.

If he told her she had worked a minor miracle, she'd just shake her head and give that blasted skirt the credit. And all the while, it was…Chelsea.

He was in love with her. Even as he admitted it to himself, a flood of sensations swamped him—a tightness in his throat, a strange pressure near his heart and a sharp sinking sensation in his stomach. The same sensations he'd been experiencing since he'd first seen her in that restaurant with Daryl's head up her skirt.

He was getting used to it. Almost.

He intended to do something about it. He'd gotten the ring—his mother's—out of the safe in his apartment the moment he'd gotten back from the hospital. He'd planned on going to her apartment after the ball… Now, he had to change his plans. But he was still going to ask her tonight—just as soon as he could get her away from this place—right after the stroke of midnight when it was officially Christmas Eve. Both of them had memories to replace.

AFTER SIXTY straight seconds of dancing with Jerry McDaniels, Chelsea had decided two things. First of all, Zach's brother was about as smooth on the dance floor as the Tin Man from the *Wizard of Oz*. Second, and more important, the skirt was having no effect on him. No doubt after the full day she'd put it through, it was worn out again. Congressman McDaniels seemed determined not to even talk to her. Instead, he was exchanging pleasantries with any other couple who came within range. Since he was a whole foot taller than she was, she didn't get in his way at all.

Glancing past Jerry's shoulder, she caught Miranda's encouraging wink and Daryl's thumbs-up. Beyond them, she saw Zach leaning against one of the drink stations chatting with a pretty, blond bartender. Shifting her gaze to Jerry, she decided to be blunt.

"Why don't you want your brother to run *Metropolitan*?" Jerry missed a step and Chelsea watched the friendly politician's smile disappear. He started to frown, then caught himself. But he wasn't ignoring her anymore.

"That's none of your business, young lady."

"No, it's not," she agreed. "But it seems to me that it's bad business for you to want to remove him."

"It's my duty. He's going to ruin a magazine my father spent a lifetime building."

Chelsea shook her head. "You don't believe that.

You're his brother and you know him well enough to know that he can excel at anything he sets his mind to. That's what really bugs you about him. You're jealous."

Jerry caught himself frowning again and after a quick glance around the dance floor, he laughed shortly.

"Nonsense. Zach has made nothing of his life, so there's nothing for me to be jealous of."

"Oh, baloney. I've got three brothers of my own, and I know all about sibling rivalry. I've never been able to please my stepfather. They please him whatever they do. I had a tough time dealing with that until I figured out that it was ruining my relationship with them. They're not bad kids and I was blaming them for something that was their father's problem."

This time Jerry forgot to prevent the frown. "It's not the same. He wasn't my stepfather."

Chelsea met his eyes. "That's got to make it even worse. At least mine had the excuse that I wasn't really his own child."

They weren't dancing anymore, but Chelsea didn't think Jerry was aware of that. "That's not what I mean," he said. "Zach's got no business printing the kind of articles you write. It's not the direction my father wanted the magazine to go in. It's my duty to ask the board to remove him."

"But Zach agrees with you. He never wanted to print my articles. He's only doing it to honor the contract that Esme Sinclair had me sign."

"Wait," Jerry paused to run a hand through his hair. "You're saying that Esme is the one who bought the articles from you?"

Chelsea nodded. "But someone wants to stop the articles as much as you do. Someone tried to run Zach and me down. They've been making threatening phone calls and sending notes. Then my apartment was ransacked and this morning someone knifed Zach."

"Zach was knifed?" Jerry asked, his frown deepening. "You're not making this up?"

"He's got fourteen stitches in his arm. Will that convince you? I can take you right over to him and you can count them."

But Jerry wasn't listening to her. Chelsea could see that he was looking around the ballroom, searching for someone.

"Zach's right over there by the drink station," she said.

"Mind if I cut in?" Daryl asked.

"Mmmm?" Jerry glanced at him.

"I'd like to dance with Chelsea," Daryl said. "The two of you have stopped. It seemed like a good time to ask."

"Go ahead." Jerry put a hand on Chelsea's arm. "I want to thank you, Ms. Brockway. For setting me straight about Zach before I—I may have made a mistake. Please, excuse me."

"Something's bothering him," she said as Jerry moved past them and began to thread his way through the other couples on the floor. She had time to notice that he wasn't headed in Zach's direction before Daryl pulled her into his arms.

"Yeah, well from the daggers that your beau was sending his way, he's probably suffering from internal bleeding."

ZACH FELT a little of his tension ease when Jerry walked off the dance floor. His parting from Chelsea had seemed amicable enough, but he didn't look happy now.

"I've had my reservations about you, but getting Ms. Brockway to sweet talk your brother is one smooth move."

It took Zach a second to realize that the comment had been addressed to him and he turned to find Bill Anderson at his side.

"I can't take the credit for that. It was my aunt Miranda's doing," Zach said.

Bill shrugged. "My daddy used to say that the next best thing to having good ideas was surrounding yourself with people who would give them to you."

For a moment Zach said nothing. Then he gave Anderson a brief nod. "I'd say your daddy had a point."

For a moment the two men merely studied each other. Finally, Bill said, "I think I was wrong about you. I was sure after that first staff meeting that you were hell-bent on taking the magazine off in a new direction without paying any attention to any of us. I figured when you finished your little experiment, you'd move on and leave the rest of us to pick up the pieces."

"What makes you think you were wrong?"

"Because you're loyal and you're honest. You honored Ms. Brockway's contract when you can't have wanted to."

Beyond Anderson's shoulder, Zach could see that Jerry had stopped to chat with Esme Sinclair.

"And you're sticking by her even though it can't be what you want for the magazine."

"It might not matter what I want for *Metropolitan* after the board meets."

Bill followed the direction of Zach's gaze. "Don't underestimate Ms. Brockway's persuasive power. I changed my mind about resigning that first day because of her. And once Esme tells your brother about the sales figures on the latest issue, he'll most likely reconsider his plan to urge the board to accept your resignation."

"What sales figures? The first issue under my tenure just hit the streets yesterday."

Bill studied him for a minute. "No one told you? Your first issue of *Metropolitan* is well on its way to selling out. I assumed Esme must have let you know by now. The distributors have been flooded with calls for more copies ever since Ms. Brockway's appearance on that TV talk show."

"Did Esme tell you this?" Zach asked glancing beyond Bill's shoulder to check on Chelsea again. She was still dancing with Daryl.

"No. I took some calls yesterday afternoon after everyone had cleared out. I just figured she must have known because earlier calls would have been routed to her office. But not to worry. I contacted our printers, and they promised to ship everything they had to our distributors first thing Tuesday morning. The last shipments ought to be hitting the stores and newsstands just about the same time you finish up on *Good Morning, New York*. Another great idea by the way."

"That one wasn't mine either," Zach said in a wry tone.

Bill Anderson was chuckling when Zach saw Hal Davidson tap Daryl on the shoulder. "You'll have to excuse me," he said as he strode toward the dance floor. He saw Sam moving in from the other side of the dance floor, but he reached them first.

"My turn," Zach said. Then before Hal Davidson had a chance to reply, he took Chelsea's hand in his and led her away.

"When you cut in, you're supposed to dance," Chelsea muttered as they threaded their way between couples.

"I'm not dancing with you," Zach said. "I shouldn't even be close to you."

She stopped then and faced him. "Why not? I don't have cooties, you know."

"You—" Zach stopped short and blinked. "Cooties?"

"You know. They're little bugs that crawl all over

you—they live in your hair, in your ears." Before he could anticipate it, she reached up and twisted his ear.

"Ouch!"

"Since you're not going to dance with me, I'm going to dance with Hal."

"No, you're not." Grabbing her hand again, he led her through one of the wide arched exits from the ballroom.

"Where are we going?" Chelsea asked.

"As soon as Sam follows us out here, you're going home."

"I am no—"

He silenced her by grabbing her close for a quick, hard kiss. "Don't you understand. Sam says that the knifer was clearly after me. It's not safe for you to be anywhere near me."

Chelsea stared at him. "That's why you've been avoiding me? To protect me?"

"Yes. Now will you go?"

But she was pulling him along the corridor, trying doors. When she found one that opened, she pulled him through it, then flipped the switch. He had time to notice that it was a storage closet before her arms were around him, her mouth pressed against his.

"That was a rotten thing to do," she said when she drew back to let him breathe, to let them both breathe. "I hate you." But her arms were around his neck, her fingers threading through his hair. "I thought you didn't want me."

"I wanted you," he said as he rained kisses along her jaw, down her neck. "And I want you now."

"I know," she murmured as she nipped at his ear.

"But we can't." He struggled for control.

"We can," she corrected, drawing his mouth to hers, and whispering against his lips. "Here. Now."

Sensations flooded through him as her mouth moved on his, her tongue probing. Her heat, her scent, her taste, swirled in his head until he couldn't separate them. All night long he'd watched her in other men's arms. Now she was his. Slipping his fingers beneath the thin straps on her shoulder, he began to push them aside.

"No." She drew back, pushing against his chest. "You can't."

Zach tried to clear his head. "But you just said—"

"I just mean that you can't take off my top. Daryl sewed me into it. If you loosen it, my skirt won't stay up."

"Damn the skirt," Zach said. "I want to touch you. I've been waiting to touch you all day. And you dragged me into this closet...."

"To have my wicked way with you." Taking his hands, she kissed one palm and then the other. "It's just the top you can't mess with. I have to be able to walk back out there and face your aunt and everyone else. So do you."

"This is crazy," he murmured as he laid his forehead against hers for a moment. He thought of his plans for making love to her, of asking her to marry him. When the ball was over, he reminded himself. When it was safe. "Am I ever going to be able to plan anything where you're concerned, Chelsea Brockway?"

"You did a pretty good job last night in that chair," she reminded him.

"Only *pretty good*?" he asked as he gripped her waist and lifted her onto a low, narrow shelf.

"I'm sure with practice, you could improve."

His mouth cut her off then, pressing hard and hot against hers. She'd meant to continue teasing him, but his hands were finally where she wanted them, brushing up along her thighs, pushing the skirt out of the way. Whatever thoughts she'd had, whatever words she'd intended to say gave way to arrows of heat and pleasure. She tightened her grip on his shoulders, moaning softly. When his knuckles brushed between her legs, she arched against his hand, helpless against the sharp wave of pleasure. Then he hooked his fingers in the waistband of her panty hose and lowered them slowly, pressing his mouth to the skin he bared on her thighs, her knees, her ankles.

Heat streamed through her in wave after wave and needs built so quickly she thought they would swallow her. Then his mouth was pressed against hers again, hot and hard. She met the demand, wrapping her legs around him and pressing as close as she could get.

"Wait," he said, shifting her back to unfasten his belt and pull down his zipper. Then he was pulling her closer, positioning her legs. His fingers burned into her hips as he gripped her and pulled her forward. Finally, she felt the incredible pressure, the searing heat as he pushed into her.

When he suddenly withdrew, the emptiness was almost unbearable. Chelsea heard herself say his name, a soft throaty whisper, "Zach, please."

"You're mine. Tell me."

"I'm yours."

Zach began to move then. He'd intended to go slowly, but the words, hearing her say them as her heat closed around him made something snap. Grasping her tightly, he pushed into her faster and harder. He couldn't stop himself. In the dim light cast by the bulb hanging from the ceiling, he knew nothing but her. She was all he could see, all he could think of. She filled him until there was no one else and nothing else but the long explosion of pleasure that they brought each other.

Afterward, he held her tightly against him, for his own sake as much as hers. He was trembling. No one had ever weakened him this way. Chelsea was the first to speak.

"I think that was more than *pretty good*," she said against his shoulder.

Zach felt his laughter bubble up and break free. When she joined him, he gave her a quick hug before he drew back to look at her. "Am I ever going to be able to predict what you'll do or say next?"

"Probably." She glanced around the room. "But this was a first for me."

Zach's smile faded. "For me, too." Raising one of her hands to his lips, he said, "Chels..."

A soft knock on the door interrupted him. Swearing, he handed Chelsea her panty hose, then moved close to the door. After a moment the knock sounded again. "McDaniels?"

Recognizing Sam's voice, Zach opened the door. "What is it?"

"I wouldn't have interrupted, but your brother wants to talk to you. He was asking your aunt where you'd disappeared to and she came to me. He says it's urgent."

Zach glanced back at Chelsea and saw that she had slipped down from the shelf. The last thing he wanted to do was talk to his brother. "Ready?"

"I could use a little stop at the ladies' room," she said.

"You stick with Chelsea," Zach told Sam as they stepped into the hallway. "I'll see what my brother wants."

A QUICK LOOK in the powder room mirror told Chelsea that they hadn't ruined Daryl's creation. A smile curved her lips. Maybe later, they could try again. But for now, the tape and staples were holding. It was her hair that needed repairing. She was running her fingers through it when Esme Sinclair joined her. The woman was carrying a fur coat over her arm.

"We're going to have to stop meeting in powder rooms," Chelsea said.

Esme shot her a thin smile in the mirror as she slipped into the coat, then removed a silver lipstick case from her bag. "Yes, we do. Before I left, I wanted to congratulate you. Your articles on the skirt are even more successful than I'd hoped."

Chelsea turned to her. "I owe it all to you. If you hadn't been willing to take a chance on me... I want to thank you again for that."

Esme's smile faded. "That first day when you walked into my office, you reminded me of myself—thirty years ago."

"I'm flattered. I've always admired—" Her sentence trailed off, blocked by the fear that rose to her throat the moment she saw Esme draw a gun from her pocket.

"You should have taken the advice I gave you in the powder room at Flannery's. You made a mistake by not taking the skirt articles to another magazine."

Pushing panic down, Chelsea made herself swallow. "Why?"

The lines on Esme's face hardened, but it was the expression in her eyes that had another skip of fear running through Chelsea.

"I signed you to that contract. It was my idea. I won't allow him to get the credit. Not this time. He always took the credit."

Esme moved toward her, gesturing her toward the door with the gun. Backing toward it, Chelsea made herself concentrate on what the older woman was saying. *Not this time...always.* "What else did he take the credit for?"

"For all my ideas. He promised me that one day the magazine would be mine to run. It was just another lie. And I was fool enough to believe him because I loved him."

"You're not talking about Zach. He never promised you that you'd get the magazine."

"His father promised me and Zach's just like him. Don't make the mistake I did. Don't fall in love with him. I tried to warn you."

Chelsea's back was at the door. She could feel the knob pressing into her. "Ms. Sinclair, Zach will make sure that you get the credit for the articles."

Esme's eyes went very cold. "It's too late for that. I want the magazine. His father promised me the magazine."

This close, Chelsea could see the madness in the older woman's eyes.

"You tried to run us down that night when we were at Flannery's, didn't you?"

Esme's knuckles turned white on the gun. "You wouldn't take the advice I gave you—to take the articles elsewhere. You had the staff and McDaniels eating out of your hand. I panicked."

"Then you decided to try to scare me off with threatening phone calls."

"Yes, and I told Zach's brother what the articles were about, how they might negatively impact his campaign. I knew he would stir up the board. It would have worked if you hadn't gone on that TV show. Even then, I thought I could fix things by stealing the skirt. How could you finish the articles if you didn't have it? But it wasn't in your apartment. I knew then that my first plan was the only way. I had to get rid of you."

"But the man at the ice rink stabbed Zach."

"I hired him to get you both. Now I have to do it myself." Esme grabbed her arm and pulled her away from the door. "We're going to walk to the elevator together. I'll have the gun in my pocket. If McDaniels tries to stop us, you'll convince him that we're going off to have a nightcap. Otherwise, I'll shoot him."

She would, too. Chelsea could see it in her eyes. Praying that they would make it to the elevator without running into Zach, Chelsea stepped out of the powder room. Sam was the first person she saw, but she ignored him as he pushed himself away from the wall. It wasn't until she saw Zach walking toward her that fear hit her like a solid blow in the stomach. Jerry was right behind him. She felt Esme stiffen.

Run. She mouthed the words as she walked toward the two men. Then she managed a smile. "Esme and I are going for a nightcap."

"I'll join you," Zach said.

"No." The word had come out more sharply than she'd intended. Brightening her smile, she took a step toward him. "Girls only." Then she turned quickly, blocking Zach with her body as she threw all her weight at Esme.

The noise of the shot echoed in her head as she felt

someone grab her and shove her hard. The floor came up fast and her head cracked against it. The last thing she saw was stars. Then the blackness swallowed her up.

"THIS ISN'T A HOSPITAL," Chelsea said, rubbing her eyes as they climbed out of the taxi. "This is Rockefeller Center." She might have dozed off, but the moonlight was pouring down and she'd have known that Christmas tree anywhere. "You promised me we were going straight to the emergency room. Your arm—" Esme's bullet hadn't hit him. As soon as she'd come to, she'd checked him out herself, but the wound in his arm had started to bleed again and the hotel doctor had cautioned them both to go to an E.R.

"It's your head we're getting X-rayed," Zach said, turning to her then. "If Jerry hadn't grabbed you..."

Chelsea could see the pent-up frustration in every line of his body, in his eyes. But she saw something else there too. Fear? Reaching up, she laid a hand on his cheek. "He did grab me and I've agreed to get another head X ray as long as you let them look at your arm."

With a sigh, Zach rested his forehead against hers. "Cut me some slack here, Chels. I've never done this before."

"You were just at the hospital this afternoon."

"That's not what I'm talking about."

"Then what?" She glanced around. The plaza was deserted. They might have been absolutely alone in the city except for an occasional car that passed by. "It's nearly two in the morning. We can't go skating."

"It's Christmas Eve. And I want—" Turning, he paced a few steps away, then turned back. "This isn't the way I planned it. Nothing is the way I've planned it since I met you."

He hurled the words at her like an accusation and her chin lifted instantly. "The *plan* was to go to the emergency room."

In two strides his hands were on her shoulders. The shake nearly rattled her teeth.

"Your arm!"

"Shut up!"

They'd shouted the words and then suddenly Zach was down on his knees. Chelsea felt hers go weak as she sank down so they were facing each other. "You're really hurt."

"It's my heart," Zach said.

She was almost certain that her own heart stopped. Then she saw the laugh in his eyes. An instant later, the sound of it rumbled up through his chest and spilled into the cold night air.

It was her turn to shake him, but it had no effect. He merely framed her face with his hands. "I love you, Chels."

This time her heart stopped for sure.

"I didn't want to tell you that in an emergency room." Digging into his pocket, he pulled out the box with his mother's ring. "I wanted to give you this here."

She said nothing. She couldn't do anything but stare at the ring—a diamond surrounded by rubies.

"Marry me, Chels."

She blinked back tears as she raised her eyes to meet his.

"Someone once told me that the best way to erase bad memories is to build new ones. I want you to have something happy to remember on Christmas Eve."

"I want that for you, too," she said as she threw her arms around him and drew his mouth down to hers.

When she finally drew back and got her breath, she said, "Pity there's not a chair around when you need it."

"Want to bet I can find a storage closet at the hospital?"

They were both laughing as they rose to walk hand in hand toward the street.

"Did I forget to say Happy Birthday?" Zach asked.

"Yes. When we're in our sixties, I'll still be reminding you of that."

With a laugh, he pulled her close. "I figured. I love you, Chels. Happy Birthday." Then he kissed her again. And though neither one of them saw it, the skirt caught the moonlight and glowed.

___Epilogue___

CHELSEA STARED at the reflection in the mirror. She barely recognized herself in the wedding dress that Daryl had designed for her. The white sequined top was a copy of the black one she'd worn to Miranda's Christmas ball, and this time it was paired with a long fall of silk that stopped at the tips of her shoes. There was no veil. A spray of white orchids was all she wore in her hair. If she hadn't been standing there with her best friends from college, she wouldn't have recognized herself.

Kate was on her right and Gwen on her left, each wearing identical versions of the outfit she'd worn to the Christmas ball. Daryl had whipped up copies of the little black sequined top and paired them with knock-offs of *the skirt*—hundreds of which were available at Bloomingdale's just in time for the New Year.

Neither of her best friends was wearing the real *skirt*. She hadn't offered it to them yet because... Her gaze shifted to her hand which held the man-magnet skirt in a death grip.

She couldn't seem to let the skirt go. Though she hadn't had any champagne, she could feel the bubbles banging around in her stomach. Lifting the skirt, she gave it a firm shake. But her fingers wouldn't release it.

"Not to worry, Chels." Kate patted her on the shoulder. "Daryl's on his way up. He'll know what to do."

"Solving fashion emergencies seems to be his specialty. He did an excellent job designing our dresses on the spur of the moment," Gwen pointed out.

"You don't understand. I have to throw the skirt to one of you," Chelsea said. "That way you can find your true love."

Gwen took a quick step back from it. "You can keep the thing."

"You shouldn't even be thinking about the skirt," Kate said. "Or about us. This is your wedding day. Zach is waiting for you. All you have to do is walk out that door and down the stairs."

"What's the problem?" Daryl breezed into the room with Miranda and Ramón in his wake. Before the door shut again, Chelsea caught the strains of the wedding march and felt another explosion of champagne bubbles in her stomach.

"I can't let go of the skirt," she said, raising her hand again and shaking it. The skirt unfurled like a flag, but remained clutched in her fist.

"Nonsense," Daryl said, grabbing it and giving it a firm tug.

Chelsea pitched forward but didn't release the skirt.

"All right," Ramón said, taking charge. "Here's the plan. Miranda, you grab me around the waist and I'll grab Daryl. Kate and Gwen, you grab onto Chelsea's

waist. On the count of three, we pull. One...two...
three!"

They pulled. And pulled. And pulled. In the reflection in the mirror, Chelsea could see the tug-of-war go
first toward Daryl, Ramón and Miranda, then toward
Kate and Gwen. But her hand simply wouldn't release
the skirt.

The door opened and once more the wedding march
swelled. "What in the world is going on here?"

They all straightened and turned to see Jerry Mc-
Daniels staring at them. "The guests are all seated. My
brother is standing at the altar waiting and the harpist
is starting the wedding march for the third time." He
paused to pin Chelsea with a frowning look. "You're
not planning to stand my brother up, are you?"

Miranda moved quickly toward him and patted him
on the chest. "Of course not. We'll be down in a minute. Chelsea's just having a little trouble with the
skirt."

"The skirt?" Jerry asked, giving it one dubious
glance.

"I can't let it go," she said, waving it again.

Jerry took a quick step back.

"I think it's psychosomatic," Daryl announced.
"Deep down she believes that Zach was attracted to
the skirt, not her. So she's afraid of losing him if she
gives it up."

"And I'm supposed to tell my brother and the guests
that?" Jerry asked.

"Of course not," Daryl said, taking Jerry's arm and

urging him toward the door. "You're going to ask your brother to come up here. He's the only one who can solve this problem."

"Absolutely not," Jerry said. "Part of my duty as the best man is to make sure that the groom does not see the bride before the wedding ceremony."

"Oh, stuff the pompous act, Jer. He can talk to her through the keyhole if that will make you feel better. Just get him up here." Once Jerry had exited, Daryl said, "Ramón, you can escort Miranda down and take care of the harpist. Tell her to play a little medley—save the wedding march until the bride reaches the foot of the stairs. Ladies." He held out an arm to Kate and Gwen, then said as he closed the door. "See you shortly, Chels."

Would he? Chelsea stared down at her hand. Her knuckles had turned white where she was clutching the skirt. Could Daryl be right? Was she afraid to let go of the skirt because deep down she was sure that it was all that Zach was attracted to? What if that were true?

As the seconds ticked by, she began to pace. It must be true and that was why he wasn't coming.

The knock on the door had her running toward it. "Zach?"

"CHELS?" He pounded on the door. She wasn't going to marry him. That was the fear that had made him race down the aisle and take the steps two at a time. "Open up, just a crack."

Next to him, Jerry drew in a sharp breath, but Zach

stopped him with one look. If it hadn't been for the fact that he owed Jerry Chelsea's life, he might have had some second thoughts about his newfound relationship with his brother. Jerry had insisted on coming back upstairs with him, citing his duty as best man. The others had followed like a parade. Daryl, Ramón, Kate, Gwen and Miranda stood in a line that trailed down the stairs. Below, in the living room of Miranda's penthouse apartment, the guests were all waiting to see if he could get the bride to join him at the altar.

And he would.

"Chels," he repeated. "Open the door."

"I can't," Chelsea said. "You're not supposed to see me before the ceremony."

"There won't be a ceremony if you don't come out."

"I will just as soon as I can let go of this skirt. I have to be able to toss it to Gwen or Kate, and I—"

"Wait," Zach interrupted. Then he drew in a deep breath as relief streamed through him until he was giddy with it. "Are you telling me that damn skirt is at the bottom of this?"

"Yes. I can't get my hand to open up and let it go. Daryl says it's all in my head."

Zach rested his head against the door and smiled. Life was never going to be dull as long as he was married to Chelsea. "Okay, here's the plan. We're both going to shut our eyes and then you're going to open the door and I'm going to take the skirt from you." Then he was going to make sure that one of her roommates took it to a city far, far away.

Shutting his eyes, he felt the door move and he closed his hand over hers the moment she poked the skirt through. Immediately, he wanted to touch more of her, to take her in his arms. But he had her now and if worse came to worst, he'd drag her down the aisle. First, he'd try another tack.

"It was never the skirt that made me want you, Chels. It was always you."

She didn't release it when he pulled.

"How can you know for sure?" she asked.

"Do you think it's because of the skirt that I offered you a job on *Metropolitan's* editorial staff?"

"No."

Zach leaned closer to the door. She had a lot more faith in herself as a writer than she did as a woman. And she'd been reluctant to take Esme's position until he'd explained that he was hiring the best defense he could find for the older woman. In spite of everything Esme Sinclair had done, he felt sympathy for her. He understood how hard it had been to please his father. He knew what it was like to dream all his life of running *Metropolitan*.

Leaning close to the crack in the door, Zach whispered, "You weren't wearing the skirt the first time I made love to you. Or the second."

"But I was wearing it the third time in that closet," she said.

How had he forgotten she could argue like a pro? "That was under duress. You twisted my ear. I did it to escape more bodily injury, not because of the skirt."

She laughed then, and Zach tightened his grip on her hand. "You're not wearing the skirt now. And I want you to kiss me, Chels."

"We can't."

"Keep your eyes shut." Widening the crack in the door, he found her mouth with his. The moment her lips parted in welcome, he felt her hand go limp. Easing the skirt out of it, he threaded his fingers with hers and with his free hand, he passed it off to Jerry.

As much as he wanted to linger, to deepen the kiss, he drew back while he still could. He was just in time to watch the skirt get passed off like a hot potato on down the line until Miranda finally took it, folded it and tucked it under her arm.

He tightened his grip on Chelsea's hand. "Are we ready to do this now?"

"There's just one problem," she said. "Now that the skirt's gone, I can't seem to let go of your hand."

Zach turned to look at his wedding party lined up on the stairs, the guests who were sending curious glances in their direction, then he met his aunt's eyes and suddenly grinned.

You'll never let her go...

He certainly wasn't going to. So what if he faced a lifetime of things never going quite the way he expected? Laughing, he pulled her from the room.

"That's not a problem. We'll just walk down the aisle together."

And to the surprise and thunderous applause of their guests, that's exactly what they did.

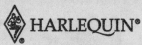